The past had finally caught up with him and he wanted it back where it belonged.

And then another stinging thought occurred—Rachel would find out too. Today and tonight had been amazing, and soon it would be spoiled when she discovered the truth.

Nikolai had never had to deal with this—a lover knowing.

And what a lover…

It would be bad enough telling his friends and seeing the distaste in their eyes, answering difficult questions. But Rachel…?

Yuri would say he was running from things, hiding things, and that wasn't Nikolai's way at all. Yet at four in the morning he went into the bedroom and picked his clothes up from the floor and dressed.

'Rachel…' His voice was not as measured as he preferred, and he had to clear his throat, but she just lay there—pretending, Nikolai was sure, to be asleep.

He didn't say her name again—he just collected his belongings and was gone.

As the door closed behind him he was almost tempted to knock and say… What? That he'd locked himself out? Or…?

No, better that she hated him than for the truth to come out, he thought as he stepped out onto the dark London streets.

Nikolai had thought he'd long ago dealt with his past.

It would seem he'd been wrong.

BILLIONAIRE
WITHOUT A PAST

BY
CAROL MARINELLI

First Published in Great Britain 2016
By Mills & Boon, an imprint of HarperCollins*Publishers*
1 London Bridge Street, London, SE1 9GF

© 2016 Carol Marinelli

ISBN: 978-0-263-26414-2

Our policy is to use papers that are natural, renewable and recyclable
products and made from wood grown in sustainable forests. The logging
and manufacturing processes conform to the legal environmental
regulations of the country of origin.

Printed and bound in Great Britain
by CPI Antony Rowe, Chippenham, Wiltshire

Carol Marinelli is a Taurus, with Taurus rising, yet still thinks she is a secret Gemini. Originally from England, she now lives in Australia and is the single mother of three. Apart from her children, writing romance and the friendships forged along the way are her passion. She chooses to believe in a happy-ever-after for all, and strives for that in her writing.

Books by Carol Marinelli

Mills & Boon Modern Romance

Irresistible Russian Tycoons

The Price of His Redemption
The Cost of the Forbidden

Playboys of Sicily

Sicilian's Shock Proposal
His Sicilian Cinderella

The Chatsfield

Princess's Secret Baby

Alpha Heroes Meet Their Match

The Only Woman to Defy Him
More Precious than a Crown
Protecting the Desert Princess

Empire of the Sands

Banished to the Harem
Beholden to the Throne

The Secrets of Xanos

A Shameful Consequence
An Indecent Proposition

Visit the Author Profile page at millsandboon.co.uk for more titles.

PROLOGUE

NIKOLAI ERISTOV HAD dealt with his difficult past.

Or rather he had been quite sure that he had.

Yet this morning, after his preferred strong tea had been poured by his butler, Nikolai did not reach for the cup as he usually would—he could not be sure that his hand would not shake, and he had long ago decided to never let another person glimpse his weakness.

It was how he had come to survive.

With breakfast served, his butler went to leave the sumptuous master suite on the bridge deck of the superyacht but Nikolai called him back.

'I need you to take care of something for me this morning.'

'Certainly.'

'I need a new a suit.'

'Savile Row and Jermyn Street are—'

'No,' Nikolai interrupted. The butler had misunderstood his request. Nikolai did not want one of London's finest tailors to be brought to the yacht, neither did he want to go and visit them. 'I want you to go to a department store and purchase a suit for me. You have my measurements.'

'I do, but—'

Nikolai gave a brief, impatient shake of his head. He did not need to explain his thinking to his butler so instead he stated his requirements. 'I want you to purchase a charcoal suit and I also need a shirt and tie that would be suitable to wear to a church wedding. Oh, and I shall need shoes too.'

'You want me to buy you clothes off the peg?' his butler carefully checked, and well he might—Nikolai was tall and broad shouldered and dressed exquisitely. His outfits came from top designers—all of whom wanted him wearing their name, just for the chance that his dark, brooding good looks would be photographed in one of their creations. Why on earth would he send his butler to a department store when his dressing room was lined with the best of the best?

'Yes,' Nikolai said, 'and I need you to go soon. The wedding is at two.'

Nikolai then told him the price range that he had in mind for his outfit and he saw his usually impassive butler blink—after all, the champagne that had been in the empty bottle he had removed from the bedside that morning had cost only a little less than had been allocated for today. That said, Nikolai spent thousands on champagne. Still, for him, it was a modest budget indeed.

'I wasn't aware that it was that time again and so soon!' The butler made a small joke and, given it was late spring, Nikolai conceded a small smile.

For a couple of months each year his life of luxury living aboard a superyacht ceased and Nikolai worked on the huge icebreakers in the Atlantic. He had recently returned. There he wore thick layers and an *ushanka*. The rest of the time he wore his wealth well. He was rich, successful in many endeavours and, Nikolai had been sure, the ghosts of yesteryear had long since been laid to rest. No one could have guessed his dirt-poor origins or the shame and fear that had used to wake him at night in a drench of cold sweat.

'Am I to purchase a wedding gift?' The butler asked.

'No.'

Only when his somewhat bemused butler had left to carry out his instructions did Nikolai pick up the cup from the saucer. He had been right to wait for his butler to leave for, yes, his hand shook slightly as he pondered how best to face this difficult day in what had once been a difficult life.

It was a good life now.

He had fought hard for it to be just that.

Nikolai had battled against the odds and had refused to become another statistic. Instead of allowing his abuser to break him, he had fought not just to survive but to thrive. Instead of turning to drink or drugs to dim the pain of the past, he had faced it.

Dealt with it.

Of course he had, Nikolai told himself.

Now he owned a fleet of superyachts and his presence was regularly requested at A-list events—a party on his yacht was *the* place to be.

He had it all, thanks to Yuri, who had been both his mentor and his saviour.

How Nikolai would kill for one more conversation with that man. How badly he needed his advice today.

The only person who knew the truth about his past had been Yuri.

'Beris druzhno ne budet gruzno,' he had told Nikolai.

It was an old Russian saying—if you share the burden it won't feel so heavy.

Nikolai had only told the truth so that Yuri would not alert the authorities who would have sent him back to *destky dom*, the orphanage from where he had run. But, as it had turned out, Yuri had been right—with the burden shared he had felt lighter.

But Yuri wasn't here and so Nikolai had had to turn to himself to work out how best to deal with today.

Nikolai wanted to see his friend married but he did not want to be seen. No doubt Sev would, if he saw him, ask why he had run away without a word to his friend and that was something Nikolai did not want to discuss.

His past must not taint his present, Nikolai had decided. He would slip into the church unnoticed and leave the same way. There was nothing he needed to do, no secrets he needed to reveal.

A small knot of disquiet tightened in his chest as Nikolai could almost hear Yuri refute his handling of the matter.

Yuri would say that by hiding, by slipping into the back of the church, he was taking the easy way out, and that was not like Nikolai.

He stood and walked across the suite and looked out to Canary Wharf, where he had docked last night. The glass was treated to ensure no one could see in—a necessary measure, for the press would love to capture images of the rich and famous and of the decadent goings-on on board his yacht. He stared out, unseen, at families and couples who were pointing and taking pictures of the attraction that his home was.

Nikolai was used to it.

His yacht was named *Svoboda*, the Russian word for

freedom and it drew crowds whenever it docked, especially as it housed its own car and the sight of the ramp opening and Nikolai driving out was impressive. More often than not his home was docked in more glittering surroundings. The south of France was a favourite, as was the Arabian Gulf.

It had been there, cruising down the Gulf of Aqaba, that Nikolai had first found out about Sev and Naomi. Lying in bed, unable to sleep, he had considered waking the blonde beauty beside him in his usual way but instead he had got up and headed up to the sundeck and, under the stars, had opened up his laptop.

As he often did, Nikolai had looked for news of his friends from *detsky dom* days and he had read the latest news about Sev.

The New York City–based Internet security expert, Sevastyan Derzhavin, was spotted in London sporting a black eye and a nasty cut. With him was his personal assistant, Naomi Johnson, wearing a huge black diamond ring on her engagement finger.

The picture that had accompanied the small piece was of Sev and, presumably, Naomi, walking hand in hand along the street, and, despite the mess of his face, Sev had looked happy.

He deserved to be.

Growing up, Sev had been the closest thing to family that Nikolai had ever known.

In the orphanage, there had been four dark-haired, pale-skinned, dark-eyed boys who had challenged the carers. They had been born with no hope but all had had dreams.

At first they had dreamt that one day they would be chosen by a family.

They never had been, though, and finally they had been cruelly told why. Their pale skin, which didn't turn pink, and their dark hair had meant they were black Russians and far harder to place than blond, blue-eyed children.

Still they'd dreamt.

The twins, Daniil and Roman, would become famous boxers, the boys were all sure. Sev, with his clever mind, would go far, and as for Nikolai, though he had no idea who his parents were, he was certain his father had been a sailor.

Certain.

Nikolai's love of the ocean had been born into him long, long before he had even glimpsed the sea.

But in *detsky dom* dreams had died easily.

At twelve years of age Daniil *had* been chosen and placed with an English family. His identical twin, Roman, had then run wilder than ever before and had been moved to the secure wing.

At fourteen, as Sev had started to shine, he had been moved to a different class and hope had been high that he would receive a scholarship to a prestigious school. Nikolai and Sev had still got the bus to school together and they'd shared a dormitory at night, but without his friend Nikolai's grades had slipped and he had been singled out by a teacher he'd loathed.

'Tell me, Nikolai, why your grades have suddenly gone down?'

Nikolai had shrugged. He hadn't liked this teacher,

who had always picked on him and given him deten-
tion, which had meant he would miss the bus and have
to walk.

'Was Sevastyan helping you?' the teacher asked.

'Nyet.' He shook his head. 'Can I go now? Or I will
miss the bus.'

It was cold and snowing and his coat was not a good
one.

'We need to discuss this,' the teacher said. 'It would
not look good on your friend's scholarship application if
I had to write that Sevastyan had helped you to cheat.'

'He didn't.'

The teacher got out a maths exam paper Nikolai had
recently taken and told him to sit and then asked him
to write the answers to the questions.

'You could do this maths two months ago, so why
not now?'

'I don't know.'

'This could be very bad for your friend...'

Nikolai stared at the numbers and pleaded for the answer to come to him. Of course Sev had helped him, it
hadn't felt like cheating, just a friend helping a friend.

And it could now cause trouble.

'Did Sevastyan do your work for you?' the teacher
asked, and raised his hand. Nikolai thought he was
about to be smacked upside the head but the man's hand
came down on Nikolai's shoulder.

'Nyet,' Nikolai said, and tried to shrug the hand off,
but it remained.

'Come on, Nikolai,' the teacher said, and, removing
his hand, he took the chair beside Nikolai. 'How can I
help you if you don't tell me the truth?'

'He didn't do my work.'

'Then you should be able to do the maths.'

Yet he couldn't.

He heard the horn blare from the bus and he knew it was leaving.

'I'll drive you home,' the teacher said, and Nikolai frowned as he would rather walk in the snow. 'About Sevastyan helping you...'

'We weren't cheating,' Nikolai pleaded, to save his friend from losing his scholarship. 'Sev just showed me how.'

'It's okay,' the teacher said gently, and Nikolai did not understand the strange tone to the man's voice yet the hammering of his heart warned him to fear it. 'We can keep it between us. Nobody has to get into trouble.'

Nikolai stared at the sums and then he felt a hand high on his thigh.

'Do they?' the teacher checked, and Nikolai didn't answer.

His butler duly returned and managed not to raise an eyebrow at the table Nikolai had upended in rage at the memory of what had taken place long ago. Instead, the butler laid out the clothes he had purchased and since neatly pressed.

Nikolai headed to the shower and decided against shaving. His thick dark hair fell into perfect shape.

He pulled on the crisp white shirt and gunmetal-grey tie his butler had chosen. The dark suit sat on his broad shoulders far better than he had expected it to.

He felt as if he were dressing for a funeral such was his grief for his lost friend, yet he wanted to see Sev happy so badly.

His eyes would remain behind dark glasses, Nikolai

decided as he put them on. He would take them off at the last moment as he stepped into the church.

He would arrive and leave unnoticed, and so, instead of summoning his driver or making a spectacle of unloading the car, he disembarked on foot and walked along South Quay then hailed a black cab.

The driver chatted about how warm the weather was for May but Nikolai did not respond. As they pulled up at the church and the driver turned for his fare, Nikolai shook his head.

'Two minutes,' he said with a heavy Russian accent.

Those two minutes turned into ten but the driver did not argue given the amount of cash that had just changed hands.

Nikolai sat watching the guests milling on the steps of the church and braced himself to head inside. The press were there and police were keeping the crowd on the other side of the road.

Sev, he guessed, must already be inside because, despite scanning the crowd, he could not make out his old friend. Sev had been an introvert and more into books and computers than people, yet on his wedding day there were many people there to celebrate.

Including Nikolai.

He watched as a tall, slender woman with a blaze of long red hair climbed out of a luxury vehicle. She was laughing and chatting as she helped a heavily pregnant woman get out. Nikolai recognised the pregnant woman as Libby, Daniil's wife, from a news article he had read during the times he had looked up his friends.

So Daniil must be here also.

The two women walked up the steps and went into

the church and Nikolai could hear the bells ringing out as others started to head inside.

'Two more minutes,' he said again to the driver.

It was proving every bit as hard as he had guessed it would be to face his past.

Sev had enquired as to the reason for Nikolai's tears on the night he had run away. Nikolai had not been able to answer the question then and he was nowhere near ready to answer it now. He did not want to see the discomfort in anybody's eyes as he revealed the sordid past.

He climbed out of the cab and walked to the church, and just as the bride's car came into view he slipped into the church.

Hopefully unseen.

Yuri, were he alive, might say he was hiding and that he should face things in his usual bold way, but on this occasion Nikolai did not want to ponder sage advice—he would take his own.

There was no need to discuss his past.

No need to re-invite shame.

CHAPTER ONE

'RACHEL, I JUST don't understand.'

Libby was clearly perplexed by Rachel's shocking news that, after a long tour of Australasia, she had left the dance company. The two women had, until recently, not only danced with the same company but had also been flatmates. Last year, just before she had met her now husband, Daniil, Libby herself had retired.

In truth, Libby had been pushed into the decision and Rachel could well remember her friend's struggle to let go of the career she loved so. They had discussed it over and over.

Rachel had made up her mind by herself.

They were friends but very different. Libby wore her heart on her sleeve, whereas Rachel kept hers not just buried in a deep vault but one where the key had been thrown away and wet concrete poured over it.

She let no one in.

Oh, she chatted, but it was mainly about the other person, and she flirted and dated but it was *always* on her terms.

Always.

They were in Rachel's vast suite at a luxury hotel, getting ready to attend a very prominent London wedding.

Rachel had never actually met the happy couple, she was there more to support Libby as Daniil was the best man and Libby was one week away from her due date.

Because Daniil owned the hotel, Rachel had been given an amazing suite. Anxious about sharing her news while determined to be upbeat for her friend today, Rachel had taken a long fragrant bath, with heated curlers in. It had done nothing to quell the nerves that lived permanently in her chest.

Rachel was always anxious, even if she hid it well, but now it felt as if everything was coming to a head.

The bath hadn't worked its magic and she had already been running late when Libby had arrived. Preparations had further stalled when Rachel had, oh, so casually dropped the news that she would not be returning to the dance company,

'But what will you do?' Libby asked.

'I'm not sure yet,' Rachel admitted as she started to pull the jumbo heated rollers out of her long red hair. 'I intend to work it out over a lot of long lazy evenings and morning lie-ins!'

'I don't get how you can have left without having made any plans. I thought you were happy…'

'I was happy. I still am,' Rachel said, and then she promptly changed the subject by going into her overnight bag and pulling out a burnt-orange velvet dress. 'What do you think?'

'It's very…' Libby's voice trailed off as Rachel squeezed herself into her very tight dress, but as she slithered it down past her thighs she frowned as she looked over and saw the pained expression on Libby's face.

'You cannot go into labour today,' Rachel warned.

'I know I can't,' Libby said. 'I keep telling myself that. I just don't think the baby is listening.'

'Do you think you might have it?'

'I think I might,' Libby admitted.

'Oh, my!' Rachel grinned her toothy grin. 'How exciting.'

'How not!' Libby sighed. 'This wedding is so important for Daniil, Sev is like family to him. Sev *is* his family.'

'I'm sure you'll be fine,' Rachel said with all the authority of someone who watched an awful lot of medical dramas 'First ones take ages and ages, and anyway your waters haven't popped. Imagine if they do in the church!'

'You're such a comfort, Rachel,' Libby said, but she did smile. 'Come on, do your make-up, we have to go.'

'I'll do it in the taxi...' Rachel said, and then remembered how rich Libby was and that this wasn't the old days. Daniil's driver would take them to the church! She pulled on very high stilettos, in the same burnt-orange velvet as her dress, and they took the elevator down and then out to where the driver waited. Once seated in the plush car Rachel opened up her large bag and, very used to doing her make-up in less luxurious surroundings, she set to work on her face.

'You're ever so pale,' Libby commented, and then remembered. 'We didn't have lunch!'

They had been too busy talking!

'I didn't have breakfast either,' Rachel said, and took a chocolate éclair sweet out from the bottom of her bag and carried on doing her make-up. Off came the freckles, thanks to an amazing foundation she had newly discovered. Her reddish-blonde eyelashes were soon a long

silky black that brought out the green of her eyes. She
added some rouge and then a good dash of coral lipstick
and then peered in the hand mirror at her slightly pro-
truding teeth that had a gap in the middle. 'I'm thinking of getting braces.'

'Why?'

'I just am. Come on, you need to bring me up to
speed, I've lost track of all these Russians.' Rachel
snapped her fingers for information as she teased out
the curls in her hair. 'The groom is Sev, Daniil's friend
from the orphanage?'

'Yes,' Libby said. 'Though it might be kinder not to
refer to him as that.'

'I can be tactful!'

'Sometimes you can be.' Libby smiled.

'Tell me about the bride.'

'Her name's Naomi,' Libby said. 'She was his PA in
New York but she's actually from London.'

'What's she like?'

'I only met her briefly, she was still his PA then. We
were just on our honeymoon. Oh, Anya will be at the
wedding too.'

'Anya?'

'Tatania.' Libby gave Anya's stage name and watched
as Rachel let out a little squeal of delight. Anya too had
been at the orphanage, though as the cook's daughter.
Now, she was prima ballerina in a Russian dance company and back in London performing *Firebird*. Rachel
had seen her the last time the company was here and
had been hoping to see her again before the production
closed next week but it was proving impossible.

'Do you think she can get me tickets?' Rachel asked.
'It's completely sold out.'

'She probably can but I doubt that she would—Anya's not very friendly,' Libby warned.

'Oh, well, it's worth a try. What about the other one?' Rachel frowned as she tried to work it out. She knew, from what Libby had told her, that there had been four orphans but she struggled to keep up with their names. 'Nikolai?'

'No!' Libby quickly said as she winced at the potential faux pas. 'Nikolai's the dead one. He killed himself when he was fourteen. He was being abused by his teacher.'

'Oh.'

Rachel answered with her usual shallow response yet she saw her own rapid blink in the small hand mirror when she heard what had happened to Nikolai.

Yes, there were things she didn't discuss, especially not on a wedding day with her anxious, pregnant friend.

Especially ever.

'You're talking about Roman,' Libby said, 'Daniil's twin. He's—'

Rachel turned as Libby broke off in mid-sentence and went silent.

'Are you having another one?' Rachel asked as they pulled up outside the church.

'No.' Libby shook her head. 'Maybe,' she admitted, as Rachel helped her out of the car. 'God, Rachel, don't let me make a scene. I can't spoil the wedding.'

'Oh, you shan't. I'll just throw a coat over you or something.' Then she smiled. 'You'll be fine.'

The bells were ringing out and the press were taking photos of the arriving guests as they walked into the gorgeous old church. There were white roses everywhere and the organ was playing. Rachel followed

Libby to a pew near the front and there was a buzz of anticipation all around.

Rachel *loved* weddings and this was going to be a good one, she was sure.

Daniil was dead sexy and the groom was too, Rachel thought, which hopefully meant half the congregation would be.

She turned and watched as a reed-thin, beautiful woman slipped into the pew behind them and then tapped Libby on the shoulder.

'Libby.'

'It's lovely to see you, Anya.' Libby smiled. 'This is my friend Rachel…'

'Anya!' Rachel said, and her face was on fire, she knew, as she had an absolute fangirl moment. Rachel had been a huge fan of Tatania for years and had followed her career closely.

'I think I must have seen you perform at least ten times…' Rachel did a little count in her head. 'Actually, twelve!'

'Rachel's not exaggerating,' Libby added. 'Any time you're in London and she wasn't performing herself she was watching you.'

'I saw you in Paris when you played Lilac Fairy. I'm hoping to get to see *Firebird* again,' Rachel said, but Anya shook her head.

'We close next week.'

'Yes, I know. I haven't been able to get tickets,' Rachel said, and let out a dramatic sigh, hoping, *hoping* that Anya would come to a fellow dancer's rescue.

'It sold out ages ago.'

Dismissed by Anya, Rachel turned and stared ahead. She could feel Libby trying not to laugh at Anya's cool acceptance of Rachel's desire to see her and her absolute shutdown with no offer of tickets!

'Told you,' Libby said.

'You did.' Rachel sighed.

As they waited for the bride to arrive Libby tried to chat about Rachel's work, or lack of it.

'You know that I've got a temporary teacher to fill in for me,' Libby said, 'but I'm always on the lookout—'

'Libby,' Rachel broke in. 'I don't want to teach.'

'Then what will you do?'

'I'm not sure.'

Her mother had asked her the same question last night with the addition of, 'I warned you to have something to fall back on.'

Rachel had said nothing at the time but her jaw had gritted. Her mother hadn't, Rachel was sure, meant another career. Evie Cary fell back onto men. Over and over. All had had money. Evie made sure that the men she dated would keep her in the style she'd like to become accustomed to.

There had been a parade of boyfriends and lovers. Some had lasted a weekend, some a few months. One for a couple of years.

He had walked out on her mother two weeks after Rachel had left home.

Surprise, surprise.

Rachel jerked her mind away from dark memories and tried to focus on the future.

She didn't need someone or something to fall back on, she wanted to fall *into* her new life.

Money wasn't too much of a problem in the short term. She had worked too hard to spend much and could take some time to figure things out. She looked over at Libby and wondered whether to tell her her idea.

'I was thinking of starting a blog.'

'A blog?' Libby said. 'Why?'

'It doesn't matter.'

The pews continued to fill, but to the right and not so much to the left, and it suddenly dawned on Rachel that, given the groom was an orphan…

Libby laughed again as Rachel's shoulders sagged.

'I thought the place would be teeming with sexy Russians,' Rachel sighed.

'Oh, well, there's always André,' Libby said.

'No.' Rachel shook her head as Libby spoke of Rachel's long-term colleague and occasionally intimate friend. 'Didn't I tell you? He's met someone and it's serious.'

'Really?'

'Yep.' Rachel nodded. 'They're getting married in a fortnight.'

'How didn't I hear this?'

'It only just happened.'

'Well, that's one wedding you'll be avoiding,' Libby said.

Rachel didn't comment and neither did she tell Libby that it was a wedding she couldn't avoid. Instead, she looked through the order of service and deliberately tried not to think about André.

'So who's he marrying?' Libby asked, and Rachel longed for Libby to have a sudden contraction, for the bride to arrive, for anything other than give the answer.

It wasn't something she wanted to talk about.

There was more.

Of course there was.

The Cary family had more skeletons in their closets than a graveyard.

'Rachel?' Libby pushed for her to answer the question but thankfully there was a stir in the congregation and Daniil said something to Sev in Russian in a shocked voice. At first Rachel assumed the bride had arrived so she turned around.

Oh, my.

Someone as good looking as this man should perhaps have known that he wouldn't be able to slink into the church unseen.

Tall with dark wavy hair that was worn a touch too long, he caused a stir simply by walking in. Heads had turned.

'Who,' Rachael asked Libby, in a voice that had suddenly gone husky, 'is that?'

'I don't know,' Libby said. 'It might be…' Her voice trailed off and Rachel watched as Libby frowned and looked over to the altar, where her husband and the groom stood. Rachel's gaze followed.

Daniil looked stunned and Sev, the groom, who had been staring ahead, had turned around at Daniil's instruction.

The shock on their faces was evident and Rachel watched as the two men broke with protocol and strode down the aisle towards this delicious stranger. Everyone was standing now, trying to get a better look. Rachel was on tiptoe, trying to make things out, but she couldn't.

'What's happening?' Rachel asked.

The only person not paying full attention was Libby.

'I'm having another one,' she moaned, and clutched at the pew.

'They're miles apart,' Rachel said in an authoritative tone to keep Libby, who was rather neurotic, calm. Libby, like all dancers, was very body aware, which meant, of course, that every freckle was cancer, every abdominal cramp in advanced pregnancy was labour…

Yikes!

Rachel was starting to stress herself, not that Libby would ever know it.

'The bride's just arrived.' Rachel kept up a running commentary as Libby breathed through the pain. Now that Naomi was here, Rachel assumed that normal services would resume but, no, the groom had brought his bride-to-be over and was now introducing her to this mystery guest.

It was all rather fascinating, Rachel thought, and a brilliant start to the wedding, especially as the bride and groom were sharing a passionate kiss, but at the wrong end of the church.

'Sev's getting off with the bride,' Rachel said. 'And I think…'

And then she was silent because Daniil had brought the delicious stranger to sit with them.

He was so tall and broad that as he moved into the pew, Libby, who wanted to keep her place near the edge in case she needed a speedy exit, had to shrink back to let him past.

Rachel did the same and got the deep woody trace of his scent as he took his place beside her.

Oh, my!

He must be Roman, Rachel thought.

But, no, that wasn't right. This guy was tall and dark but he didn't look like Daniil, and weren't he and Roman supposed to be identical twins?

She really couldn't keep up.

'Libby,' Daniil said, as the vicar called for order and for the groom to release the bride from his embrace so they could get the service under way. 'This is Nikolai, he'll sit with you.'

Now things really were getting confusing, Rachel thought.

'Don't let him leave,' Daniil added, and Rachel suppressed a smile.

Oh, she happily wouldn't let him out of her sight.

Everyone stood as Sev and Naomi walked down the aisle hand in hand and Rachel frowned as she tried to work it out.

She turned and looked up at the man next to her.

He had black wavy hair and dark velvet brown eyes that did not turn at the awareness of her curiosity.

And Libby was right again—Rachel could be rather tactless at times.

'Sorry.' Rachel frowned as she peered at him and then gave a small shake of her head. 'But now I'm really confused. Aren't you the dead one?'

CHAPTER TWO

NIKOLAI DIDN'T ANSWER her question.

Yet that Sev had thought him dead had shaken him to the core.

In a brief exchange with his long-ago friend he had found out that Sev and Daniil had thought that he had killed himself and that Sev had thought it had been his fault.

Nikolai had just glimpsed the burden he had unwittingly placed on his friend and was in no mood to respond to Miss Curiosity's question.

'I'm Rachel,' she offered.

'I think we're supposed to be paying attention to the service.' Nikolai's response was terse.

His voice made her want to say *pardon*, just for the chance to hear him repeat himself. It was deep and low and his accent so rich it made her toes curl. Rachel turned to Libby and they both frowned and pulled confused faces at each other.

There were so many questions but no time to answer them as they were now standing for the first hymn.

'You can share mine,' Rachel said generously when she saw that he didn't have an order of service.

She was like a wasp hovering, Nikolai thought.

He had wanted to just see the service and leave.

And he would still do so, Nikolai decided.

He could not face the questions.

Or, worse, answering them.

'Are you okay?' he heard her say, and then realised that the question had not been aimed at him.

'I'd better be!' Libby responded with grim determination. 'Stick close to me, Rachel.'

And then he felt, or rather heard, the woman beside him—Rachel—laugh.

It was an odd and unexpected reaction to an escalating situation and for some reason he almost smiled.

The fragrance she was wearing was possibly the scent of lying in a flower-drenched meadow in summer, not that he ever had, but Nikolai then decided that she was more like a bee.

Except her too-close proximity didn't have the threat of a sting.

He looked at the pale hands that held the paper in front of him and it was the most pointless sharing ever because neither of them was singing.

'Is she having pains?' Nikolai asked.

'Yes,' Rachel said as the hymn ended and they took their seats. 'But they're ages apart.'

Her dress rode up as she took a seat and he was treated to a glimpse of freckly white thighs, and then he watched her fidget as she pulled her dress down.

And then there was another fidget as she went into her bag and took out some toffees and offered Libby one, but she shook her head.

He watched as the gold-foil-wrapped sweet was offered to him.

'We're not at the movies,' he pointed out. Yet, again,

even in uncomfortable circumstances he had the temptation to smile. She was slightly inappropriate, yet had made herself a companion when so many had simply stared.

Nikolai had been to few weddings. His lifestyle ensured he did not get particularly close to others but seeing his friend clearly in love, he was glad he had come.

Even if he had been outed.

They stood for another hymn.

'Oh, I know this one,' Rachel said, and proceeded to sing tunelessly and loudly beside him.

She was a terrible midwife because Libby had another contraction during the second verse and, Nikolai observed, Rachel didn't appear to even notice.

He had timed them.

Rachel was right, though—they were ages apart and Libby had a while to go.

Still...

'Your friend is in pain,' Nikolai said.

'I know!' Rachel hissed, and as they took their seats while the couple went off to the vestry to sign the register she elaborated. 'Why do you think I was singing so loudly? I was trying to keep the spotlight from her.'

Rachel did not need to sing, even badly, for the spotlight to be on her, Nikolai thought. Even if he had been seated at the back of the church, his eyes would have been drawn to her. He had noticed her getting out of the car, he had seen those long pale legs as they'd climbed the church steps and that gorgeous tumble of red hair.

A harp was being played, very badly, and Rachel got back to the order of service and found that it was

Naomi's cousin who was putting the congregation through hell.

'Ouch,' she said as a note was missed, and her fidgeting resumed.

'Do you have any more sweets?' he asked.

'Always.' She smiled and went into her bag and handed him not one but two.

He unwrapped the sweet and popped it into his mouth. It was brittle, with a soft centre, and was absolutely delicious.

'Do you know why I like them?' Rachel whispered. 'They get stuck to your teeth and you can find a bit later.'

He turned then and for the first time met her eyes fully.

His were a very dark brown, almost black, Rachel thought, and his gaze was penetrating, so much so that as it shifted down to her mouth she could feel the blush of her skin.

'I'm thinking of getting braces,' she said, perhaps because they were on the subject of teeth, or perhaps just for something to say.

'Don't.'

'The invisible ones,' she amended.

'Why,' Nikolai asked, 'would you ruin such an amazing mouth?'

Oh, she was a terrible midwife because had the bride and groom not appeared then, Rachel would have been rather tempted to take his hand and simply run.

He was stunning.

She ached to see him smile, but he did not return hers and she ached for a witty retort but she had none.

The bells rang loudly and the newlyweds walked

back down the aisle and Nikolai turned his attention to them.

Daniil gave his wife a concerned look as he walked past.

'I'm fine,' Libby mouthed.

'She's lying,' Rachel muttered.

Soon they were all out on the steps and the wedding party was being arranged for photos. Nikolai knew that now was the time to leave quietly.

Yes, Sev had questions and deserved answers, but today wasn't the time for that and so, as the photographer called for everyone to gather on the steps, Nikolai walked away, hoping to disappear into the crowd.

'Hey!'

He could hear the clip of footsteps running behind him and knew who he would see when he turned around.

The bee was buzzing.

'You can't just leave!' Rachel said. She wasn't even thinking about Sev and the rest of them—more, how dare he flirt like that and simply walk off?

But Nikolai had other ideas.

'I can do exactly that,' he responded.

'You have to stay,' Rachel said. 'I've been given instructions and I take my duties as friend of the wife of the best man very seriously.'

Nikolai cared nothing about her duties and started to move away.

'It's not fair on Sev to leave,' Rachel said, and his shoulders stiffened as he halted.

'Sev's wedding is hardly the best time to catch up on things.'

'But he'll enjoy it more if you're here.' Rachel

watched as he slowly turned again. Nikolai glanced over at the wedding party and, sure enough, instead of concentrating on the photo being taken, Sev was looking in their direction, clearly wondering if Nikolai was about to disappear.

Again.

'Very well,' Nikolai conceded. 'I'll stay for the reception but then I'm going back.'

'To where?'

'To my life.'

Rachel was curious to know more. His accent was heavy and she guessed that London wasn't his base. As they started to head back to the group she asked for more information. 'And where is your life?' she asked. 'Where do you live?'

'Nowhere for long. I don't like to get too involved with any one place or person.'

He turned his head slightly and his eyes told her to step back from the conversation, to drop it.

She did so.

'There's Libby,' Rachel said, and gave her friend a wave.

Libby was clearly looking for them. 'There you are.' She smiled. 'Sev wants you in a photo, Nikolai.'

Nikolai gave a nod and walked off towards the church, and Rachel and Libby watched as the three men stood on the steps of the church. A photo was taken of them with Naomi and then the photographer called for Libby to join in.

Rachel watched Libby make her weary climb up the steps to smile widely for the camera and then Libby and Naomi stepped aside and there was a photo taken of just the three men. Rachel glanced to her side and saw that Anya was standing nearby.

'It's a shame the other one isn't here,' Rachel said, and watched as Anya frowned. 'Roman,' Rachel clarified.

'If he was here there would be trouble.' Anya shrugged. 'He would make sure of that.'

'Still, it would be nice if Daniil could find his twin.'

'Some people don't want to be found!' Anya dismissed the notion. 'Daniil should accept that fact.'

'It's his identical twin.'

'So?' Anya said. 'Sometimes you just have to get over things.'

She really was incredibly cold, Rachel thought as Anya walked off. If she hadn't seen her dance, she would have thought Anya incapable of emotion.

Except she *had* seen her dance!

And Rachel wanted to see it again.

Nikolai rode in the car with Rachel and Libby, who told him where the reception was being held.

'Your husband bought the hotel last year?' Nikolai said.

'He did.' Libby smiled. 'So you've been keeping an eye on him?'

'A bit,' Nikolai admitted. He looked over to where Rachel sat and saw that she was freshening her lipstick, and when she spoke he liked it that she had more important things on her mind than finding out about him.

'Do you think I should simply ask her?' Rachel asked Libby. 'Maybe I was too subtle in the church.'

'Rachel,' Libby said, 'I don't think anyone could ever accuse you of being subtle.' Libby turned and explained the conversation to Nikolai. 'Rachel is desperate to see

Firebird but it's completely sold out. She was hoping that Anya—'

'Anya?' Nikolai broke in, clearly recognising the name.

'I believe that she was the cook's daughter at the orphanage.' Libby nodded. 'Well, her stage name is Tatania and she now plays the lead in *Firebird*. She was standing behind you in the church.'

'She will be there at the reception?' Nikolai asked.

'She will be.' Libby nodded. 'Though only for a little while, she has a performance tonight.'

'And I'm going to ask for tickets for next week,' Rachel said as the car pulled up at the hotel. 'Just watch me.'

He was!

Given the venue and that Daniil owned it, of course things went smoothly. Nikolai's name had even been added to the table plan. He was seated beside Anya and another guest but Rachel shamelessly got out her pen and moved things around so that he now sat next to her.

'We can't have you not knowing anyone.'

Canapés and champagne were served as the guests waited to be invited into the ballroom and he took a drink as did Rachel, though again she chatted to Libby rather than to him.

He liked that. He appreciated how neither woman pounced on him for information, though possibly because they had something more pressing on their minds.

'How are you feeling now?' Rachel asked.

'I'm fine.' Libby smiled as she took a glass of sparkling water from a waiter. 'I haven't had one since the church.'

'It's probably just a little warm-up for next week,' Rachel reassured her.

'Have you rung your doctor?' Nikolai asked, and Rachel blinked at his rather assertive intrusion into what was clearly girls' talk.

'I don't think that's necessary.' Libby smiled politely and then, as she went to turn back to Rachel, she wavered and spoke to Nikolai. 'Do you?'

'It can't hurt to check.'

'I'm sure you'll be fine,' Rachel said, and shot Nikolai a look that told him not to worry her friend, but Nikolai just gave her a small shrug in response.

'Anyway, less talk of babies.' Libby tried to drag her mind from imminent birthing. 'Rachel, you still haven't told me. Who's André marrying?'

It was only then, for the very first time, that Nikolai saw the rather forward Rachel appear just a touch uncomfortable—her neck went red and she took a sip of her drink before answering.

'I don't want to talk about André.'

'Oh, come on,' Libby pushed. 'I miss all the gossip. Who is she?'

'Just someone he met when we were on tour.'

'You're not going to go to the wedding, are you?' Libby said. 'How bloody awkward would that be, given that you two were—'

'Libby,' Rachel snapped. 'Can you just drop it?'

He could see Rachel's discomfort—more than that, he could *feel* it. He watched as she almost leapt on a passing waiter, holding up her glass and asking for more champagne.

Her glass was replaced with a full one and as Rachel took a grateful sip she met Nikolai's slightly questioning gaze but thankfully they were then summoned to go through.

The ballroom looked incredible.

Dressed in shades of white, from the lavish white roses to the crisp tablecloths, it was picture perfect. The air was fragrant and as they took their seats thankfully Libby seemed to have forgotten what they had been discussing.

'Anya!' Nikolai stood as she approached and kissed her on the cheek. 'It is good to see you. I hear you are doing well.'

'I am,' Anya said, and, out of the corner of his eye, Nikolai watched as Libby and Rachel shared a small smile at Anya's arrogance.

It was a lovely meal, at least, for those who ate it.

Libby was struggling. She could barely manage to drink her water and declined an entrée, whereas Anya shook off the dressing and nibbled on a small piece of Cornish crab.

Rachel and Nikolai dived in.

'It's such heaven not to have to watch my weight,' Rachel groaned as her main course of beef Wellington was served.

Anya's meal wasn't so gleefully received and she promptly pushed her plate away.

'Is there a problem?' the waiter checked.

'No problem,' Anya responded.

Nikolai chatted in Russian to Anya and made no apology for it. It was nice to speak with her because Anya was so self-absorbed that she really asked nothing of him.

'I will have to leave as soon as the speeches are finished,' Anya explained, and then told him about her rise to the top, her career, and then Nikolai asked her a question.

'How long have you been in touch with Daniil?'

'He and Libby came and saw me perform a few months ago. Since then.'

'And what about Sev?'

'I don't really know him.'

'What about Roman?'

Anya shrugged. 'I don't spend my free time looking up people from the orphanage where my mother used to work.' She glanced at Rachel, who was sulking at being ignored as they spoke in Russian. 'You have a fan.'

'I know,' Nikolai said. The odd thing was he was fast becoming a fan of Rachel's.

'How have you been?' she asked.

'I'm well.'

'That's good.'

She was as Russian as he. No emotion on display and her indifference was soothing, though Nikolai knew that at some point, if he kept in touch, questions would come.

For now, though, there was no probing. At least, not from his left. To his right, Rachel, clearly less than impressed that his back was to her and he was speaking in Russian, was trying to squeeze into the conversation.

'Anya...' She leant forward and spoke around Nikolai. 'I have to say I really want to—'

'I'm just going to the loo,' Libby interrupted.

'Do you want me to come with you?' Rachel offered.

'Rachel,' Libby warned. 'You don't need to hold my hand. I'm fine.'

Now Anya and Rachel shared a look.

'You've seen me perform, then?' Anya deigned to address Rachel.

'Many times.' Rachel nodded. 'I'd been to see *Fire-*

bird a couple of times before you took the lead and I was very annoyed when Libby was there and I missed it.'

'Vera was annoyed too,' Anya smirked.

'Vera?'

'Atasha—the previous lead.'

'I came for your second performance,' Rachel said. 'I wrote a piece on it.'

'For who?' Anya asked.

'For me.'

Anya wasn't interested in that. Instead, she turned to Nikolai and spoke now in English. 'You should come and see me.'

Oh, so it wasn't sold out for him!

'I'm not interested in ballet,' came Nikolai's response.

They were all so rude to each other! Rachel thought.

'You should have said yes,' Rachel hissed at him. 'You could have given the ticket to me!'

'Tickets,' Nikolai said.

'Tease.'

Libby returned to her seat and it was she now who fidgeted.

'Do you think you should do what Nikolai—?' Rachel started, but Libby shot her a look.

'The speeches are starting,' Libby said.

The father of the bride went first and that was very boring, Rachel thought. Then it was Sev, who made a toast to absent family and friends and raised a glass in the direction of Nikolai. Rachel was more focused on Libby breathing rather deeply beside her. But when Daniil stood to deliver the best man's speech Rachel found that she was hanging on every word as he offered some insight into the time at the orphanage where Nikolai had been raised. She wanted to know more about the man who sat beside her. He fascinated Rachel. It was not just that he was so good looking, it was more the mystery that surrounded him and that he had offered no update to anyone on the intervening years.

'There were four of us who grew up in the orphanage,' Daniil explained. 'Sev looked out for all of us. He would try to halt an argument or tell us when to pull back. He would also read to us,' Daniil said. 'Sometimes it was a book on cooking that he had found, or gardening. One time a carer had left a sexy book...' The guests all started to laugh as Daniil explained how the boys had kept getting him to read it again and again.

Rachel looked at Nikolai but his expression gave nothing away, even when Daniil spoke about how they had all hoped for a family.

Had Nikolai hoped? Rachel wondered.

But suddenly Rachel had no choice but to lose focus on Nikolai.

'Rachel...' Libby whispered, and she dragged her mind to the reason she was here—her very pregnant friend.

'Are you okay?' Rachel checked, and then saw that Libby's eyes held urgent appeal.

'No!' Libby said. 'Follow me out in a couple of moments but, please, Rachel don't make it obvious.'

'Okay.'

She glanced at Anya, who appeared not to care—she was picking a tiny flake of chocolate off the top of a mousse and trying not to eat it!

Rachel watched as Libby attempted a subtle exit but then, just as she went to stand, a low, deep voice asked her a question. 'Did you bring gloves with you?'

Rachel found herself smiling as she turned to him. 'Er, no.'

'But you have toffees,' he pointed out.

'I do,' Rachel said. 'She can bite down on them.'

'You'd better go.'

Rachel stood, and just before heading out she bent over and whispered into his ear. 'If you hear screams—it's me.' And made her discreet exit.

Only it wasn't discreet to Nikolai.

A blaze of orange, her hair had just brushed against his cheek in their whispered conversation and it was as if he could still feel it as her scent lingered.

He watched her hitch her dress down her thighs as she walked out on very high heels.

It would be foolish to get involved, even for one night, Nikolai told himself. Women came and went with ease in his life, but Rachel was connected to the people from his past and that complication he did not need.

Daniil, having seen his wife leave, wrapped up the speeches and soon the dancing would start.

'I have to go,' Anya said to Nikolai. 'You can walk me out.'

He did, and gladly so, because now that the speeches were over he knew that soon Sev would be looking to speak with him and he was considering making his own getaway.

They came out to the sight of Rachel holding Libby up and Daniil on the phone. 'Daniil's calling the hospital,' Rachel explained, uninvited. 'And his driver's on his way.'

'I'm just calling for mine,' Anya said, and took out her own phone.

They were so reserved, Rachel thought. Most people she knew would be panicking and as flustered as she was.

Daniil looked a bit grey but that was as far as it went. Nikolai and Anya were chatting in Russian, as if a heavily pregnant woman wasn't moaning close by them.

'So,' Anya asked, 'do you think back to those days?'

'I do all I can not to think of those days,' Nikolai said. 'Why did Sev think I had died?'

'A body was dragged from the river a couple of weeks after you disappeared. Your bag had been found further upstream, with that wooden ship you built and the sexy book...'

Nikolai swallowed.

'Sev was devastated,' Anya admitted. 'He blamed himself.'

'Why would he blame himself?'

'That is what tends to happen when your closest friend throws themselves into a cold river rather than tell you there is something wrong.'

It was a difficult conversation but it did not look like it to an outsider. Rachel couldn't believe how easily Anya and Nikolai appeared to be chatting as Libby started to groan again. 'You have the oddest friends,' Rachel said as she rubbed Libby's back.

'I know they are.' Libby came out of the contraction and they both shared a smile as Anya waved over to them as her car arrived. 'I hope it goes well, Libby,' Anya said, as her chauffeur got out and opened the car door.

Libby nodded but once Anya was in the car her face moved into a snarl, which was most unlike Libby, especially what she said next. 'Tough bitch.'

'Oh, God!' Rachel exclaimed. 'You're going to have it

now, aren't you? On one of the shows I watch they start swearing...' Her voice trailed off and she saw that Daniil was waving to his driver, who was stuck at traffic lights, to hurry, and that Nikolai was walking back inside.

'Nikolai,' Rachel called out to him. 'Get here.'

He came over.

'How could you leave?' she asked.

'I am sure Libby would prefer—'

'It's not about what she might prefer,' Rachel interrupted. 'I might need some help.'

'Do you want to push?' he calmly asked Libby.

'No.'

'Then she has plenty of time till the baby arrives,' Nikolai said.

He just stood there calmly, as if slightly bored, until Daniil's driver pulled up and then asked, 'How far away is the hospital?'

'It's just five minutes away,' Libby said. 'Without traffic!'

The streets were packed.

'You'll be fine,' Nikolai said.

Daniil seemed to think so too and he shook his head when Rachel offered to climb in the back with them. 'There's no need.'

'But what if she has it on the way?' Rachel asked as she protested her dismissal.

'How many babies have you delivered, Rachel?' Daniil asked.

'Er, that would be none.'

'How about you, Nikolai?'

'Two,' Nikolai answered, and smothered a smile at Rachel's pout. 'Do you want me to come with you?' he offered.

'God, no!' Libby said.

'You'll let me know when she has it,' Rachel checked. 'I don't care what time it is!'

'Of course.' Daniil gave her a nod and then got in the back with his wife and as they drove off she turned to Nikolai.

'You took all the drama out of that, didn't you?' Rachel accused.

And then, *then* she got his smile.

His full one.

It was like a wave rushing in unexpectedly—with no buffer. He was absolutely beautiful and his smile welcomed her, for the very first time, into his space.

She stood there, late in the afternoon on a busy street, as if finally alone with him, and smiled back.

'How come you've delivered two babies?' Rachel asked, moving one step closer. 'Are you a doctor?'

'No.'

'A nurse, then?'

'Please, no.'

'Then how—?'

'I worked on ships,' Nikolai said. 'The first baby I delivered, the mother was a stowaway and they don't tend to declare they are pregnant and neither do they come with health insurance.'

'Oh, my God!' He was utterly fascinating, Rachel decided. She simply had to know more. 'Tell me!'

'The mother and baby were fine.'

'What about the other one? Was she a stowaway as well?'

'No, she was a colleague and didn't know she was pregnant. That baby was very small.'

'Did it live?'

'Yes.'

Rachel wanted to snap her fingers for more information but he told her no more.

Nikolai could feel her curiosity and impatience and he cast another slow smile in her direction.

Oh, his mouth was like a magnet because with just a small shift of his lips Rachel took a step towards him.

'I'm going to find out,' she warned him.

'No,' he said. 'You're not.'

'I'm very persistent. Just watch me.'

'I *am* watching you.'

She was tall. It had been a bane career-wise but it was a pleasure now because it meant that in high heels she was close to eye level with him. Nikolai did not move from her proximity and rare was the man who wasn't just a little bit intimidated by Rachel in seductive mode.

He was far from intimidated.

'I think the music might have started,' she said.

'Probably.' Nikolai responded, though he made no move to head back inside.

'So,' she asked, 'are you going to ask me to dance?'

She was a flirt and a very skilled one at that, but, she fast realised, she was no match for Nikolai. She expected him to shrug, or say maybe, or even to agree and ask her to dance. Instead, he answered her with a truth.

'I don't need to ask.' He took her hands and moved them so they came around his neck, then he placed his hands on her hips. 'Do I?'

They were out on the street, standing to the side of the red carpet that led to the hotel, and she swayed to no music as he stood still.

She tried to move her body in but he held her so that she could not, all she could do was look into his eyes.

He stared back at her and she had never met anybody so good at eye contact. It wasn't invasive or uncomfortable; instead, their eyes told each other secrets.

His gaze told her of his desire, and hers told Nikolai that he could kiss her now.

Please.

Yet he did not.

Instead, his eyes told her he would make her wait for that pleasure.

She moved her mouth in, just a little.

He moved his face back.

His hands were warm through her dress but nothing compared to the heat between her legs. Perhaps it was better that they did not kiss because if his mouth met hers now, she might ignite.

'We should go inside,' he said.

'Why?' Rachel asked, because she rather liked being out here with him. 'I'm not on baby watch any more.'

'We need to talk.'

'I thought you didn't want to talk.'

Usually he didn't. Their lips were almost touching but it wasn't just the feel of a mouth that he wanted— he wanted to hear her words.

'I want to talk about you—I want to know just who it is that André is marrying.'

And she smiled because it would seem that, despite his apparent indifference, he had been paying attention after all.

'That's not very fair,' she teased. 'Why would I tell you about myself when I know nothing about you?'

'I don't play fair,' he said, and she felt her heart rate quicken as he looked right into her eyes and told her that he made his own rules. 'Come on, let's go in.'

'It's going to be very loud in there,' she pointed out, more than happy to stay outside for a while longer. She wanted to find a seat, to be alone with him, rather than be dragged back into the crowd. 'Not very good for conversation.'

'We'll manage,' Nikolai said. 'We just need to get close.'

CHAPTER THREE

NIKOLAI TOOK RACHEL by the hand and they headed back inside.

The doors were held open for them as they entered the ballroom. Indeed, the music had started and, though there was an ache for physical contact, there was a need to be close on a different level.

Nikolai was not used to needing to know more about somebody. He usually preferred minimal exchange of information, yet somehow she intrigued him just as much as he fascinated her.

Why, Rachel wondered as he led her to a dark corner, was she considering telling this man something that she was struggling to tell her very best friend? Maybe it was because, unlike Libby, he had seen her discomfort about the topic of André's wedding. Rachel didn't blame Libby a bit—clearly her mind had been on other things this afternoon. Still, Rachel could just imagine Libby's reaction if, or rather when, she found out that it was her cousin Shona that André was marrying.

Libby's distaste she did not want to see.

Would she get that from Nikolai?

Rachel truly didn't know.

Still, it would be nice to get someone else's perspective. She was tired trying to work through it herself.

He called a waiter over and asked for coffee, which was served with a slice of wedding cake.

She liked it that he did not rush her to speak, that instead he watched as she peeled back the icing from the cake and picked off the marzipan.

'You don't like it?' Nikolai checked.

'No.'

He took it from her plate and as she watched his fingers tear the pale yellow dough, Rachel wondered if she might change her mind about not liking marzipan just to have him lift it to her lips.

He was shockingly attractive, not just in looks but in his measured movements and the way his eyes lifted and met hers. Instead of asking her about André, he asked about her.

'You dance professionally?' he asked.

'I do,' Rachel said. 'Well, I've actually just left the company. We dancers age terribly…'

'How old are you?'

'Nineteen,' Rachel said, and wondered if he'd get her little joke—the curve of his delicious mouth told her that he did. 'I'm thirty-two,' Rachel told him. 'You?'

'Thirty-one.'

'And not dead.'

'Nope.'

'I'm so glad.'

'So am I,' Nikolai agreed with a wry smile.

'Will you keep in touch with them?' Rachel asked. 'Now that—?'

'I don't think so.' Nikolai interrupted. 'I'm just here for tonight.'

She wanted to protest, but it wasn't her place. In truth, there was also an odd comfort that tomorrow he would be gone. She could tell him her truth and not have to face him again.

'So why are you not looking forward to the next wedding that you are to attend?'

Rachel had to pause before answering. His English, though excellent, was slightly disjointed and spoken in an accent far stronger than either Sev's or Daniil's.

'You don't have to tell me,' Nikolai said, taking her silence as discomfort, but Rachel shook her head.

'No, no.' She actually wanted to tell him. 'It's a bit...' she pulled a face '...unsavoury.'

'Do tell.'

'The groom is an ex-boyfriend of mine.'

'Okay.'

'And the bride is my cousin.'

She waited for his eyebrows to rise, or for any indication that he found that distasteful, but he just stared back at her and his impassivity allowed her to go on.

'We broke up two years ago and they met a couple of months ago. My aunt Mary and cousin Shona came and saw the performance in Singapore. Afterwards they came backstage and it was there I introduced them.'

'I see.'

'No,' Rachel said. 'You don't. He's a dancer...we tour together. We're just back from a huge tour of Australasia...'

'Do you still have feelings for him?'

'Not really,' Rachel said, 'but now and then we...' She gave a small shrug and he nodded that he understood that they still slept together. 'When we're touring and things.' Rachel gave an uncomfortable shrug.

She didn't know how best to explain how it felt to be a stranger in a new city again and again. How the hours spent dancing and performing meant you were wide awake as the rest of the world went to sleep. 'It's an odd kind of lonely.'

'I would imagine that it is.'

His understanding without judgement was refreshing. 'We shan't any more, of course,' Rachel said hurriedly, and he watched her skin burn on her neck and guessed there was something else she wasn't telling him but did not push for her to reveal it. Instead, he asked another question.

'Does your cousin know that the two of you have been lovers?'

'She knows that we once dated. I just didn't feel the need to bring Shona up to speed on my sex life during the introductions.' Rachel let out a tense breath. 'It just doesn't sit right with me. Maybe he has a thing for pasty-skinned gingers.'

Nikolai frowned. 'I don't understand your words.'

'Pale-skinned redheads,' Rachel translated, and for some reason he made her smile as he nodded that he now understood.

'I suddenly have a thing for pale-skinned redheads,' Nikolai said.

'Then you must meet my cousin!'

He smiled and so did she. That she could make a small joke about a subject so touchy to her was unexpected.

'Why did you break up?' he asked, and saw Rachel's smile fade and her eyes narrow as she debated whether or not to tell him.

'He cheated.'

'And what excuse did he give for that?'

His question had her frown deepen further, because the answer exposed her. 'Apparently I'm cold.'

'I would disagree.'

'I'm not very affectionate.'

'Nor me.'

His dismissal of her faults made her smile so she told him some more.

'He said we were never going anywhere. That I didn't want to move in with him, which was true. I'd made it clear that I never wanted to settle down or have children and things.'

Rachel didn't tell him why.

'I'd call that honest.'

She liked it that he didn't ask her to justify her reasons and so she told him some more. 'Well, he said all I wanted from him was sex and that he felt used.'

'Poor boy,' Nikolai said, and now he smiled back but so close to her mouth that she felt her lips start to tingle.

'I just find the whole situation—the thought of being at the wedding—so awkward.'

'It doesn't have to be. Just don't go to the wedding.'

'I'm expected to. If I don't go then it makes it an issue.'

'But it already *is* an issue for you.'

He said it in a very matter-of-fact voice, though his words rather dizzied her because, yes, it was an issue for her yet how could she not make it one? How could she say no to her family, how could she kick up a fuss?

'Is he the reason you resigned?'

'I didn't resign,' Rachel refuted. 'My contract was up for renewal and I could maybe have squeezed another year or two…' But then she was honest. 'He was part of the reason. Dancing was always an escape…'

'From what?'

She chose not to answer that question. Oh, Nikolai was easy to talk to but some things Rachel had learned should never be said, though a few times she had tried.

'I don't like him, Mum. He—'

'He pays for your dance lessons,' Evie had interrupted her daughter's nervous plea for her mother to intervene.

Her mother had refused to hear it.

Oh, dancing had been such an escape. A route out of her family, a ticket to heaven.

She had more than paid the price.

Nikolai didn't press for a response. Not because he wasn't interested but out of the corner of his eye he could see Sev making his way over. The temptation was to avoid Sev but instead he got up and shook hands with his old friend.

'What the hell?' Sev said in Russian.

'It's good to see you,' Nikolai said in English, which set the tone. There would be no private discussion now.

'How have you been?' Sev asked.

'I'm very well. And you don't have to worry about entertaining me tonight. I am being well taken care of…' He gestured to Rachel.

'When can we catch up?' Sev asked.

'We are now.'

Rachel was trying not to listen but she heard Nikolai's evasive answer. He revealed nothing about himself, even to his old friend. In fact, he gave the impression that at any moment he might walk off. He had done just that, Rachel realised—after the wedding he had tried to simply disappear into the crowd.

He intrigued her, terribly so. And when the mother of the bride called for Sev to come and meet a relative, Rachel could almost feel the breath of Nikolai's sigh of relief move through her.

'You need to get on,' Nikolai said to Sev. 'You're in demand tonight.

'We'll talk later,' Sev said, and Nikolai didn't answer. Instead, he gave a small nod and took his seat again next to Rachel.

'Were the two of you close?' Rachel asked.

'We were.' Nikolai nodded.

'Not now, though?'

'I haven't seen him for many years.'

'So, what do you do?' Rachel asked. 'For work?'

'I…' Nikolai hesitated. She had told him about herself after all. No, he didn't mention the fleet of yachts and ships that he owned, neither did he mention the luxurious vodka bars around the world that were in his name. Instead, he gave her just a small glimpse of his life. 'For a couple of months a year I work on the icebreakers.'

'Icebreakers?'

'They are large ships that break up the ice and open up the trade routes after winter.'

'Is it lonely?'

'Not at all.' Nikolai shook his head.

'And what do you do for the other months of the year?' Rachel asked.

'I do what I please.' That wasn't strictly true—his shipping empire, along with other business interests, was more than a full-time job, though, maybe what he said wasn't so far from the truth for it pleased Nikolai to work hard each and every day, from wherever he chose to be in the world.

'It sounds like my dream…' Rachel sighed, and Nikolai now frowned.

'You want to work on the icebreakers?'

'No!' Rachel laughed at the very idea for a moment but then she was serious. 'Working hard for part of the time and then doing what you please. I'm thinking of…' Rachel stopped. She hadn't told anyone her thoughts, not even Libby who had pushed and pushed to know her plans.

'Thinking of what?' Nikolai asked, and then watched as her vivid green eyes narrowed a touch as she considered whether or not to continue.

Tomorrow he would be gone, Rachel reminded herself. She liked his perspective and his measured responses and so for the first time she told another person her tentative plans. 'I don't want to be tied down,' she admitted. 'I know I've travelled and things but I've been so committed to dance…' It was hard to explain. 'Since I was five years old it's all I've wanted to do. Now I like the idea of doing other things…'

'Such as?'

'I like writing about dancing,' Rachel admitted, and her cheeks turned to fire, but Nikolai just sat and listened. 'I like seeing how the same performance changes night by night. The dynamics and different interpretations. I've saved up a lot and I'm wondering if I can just drift for now. Maybe travel and watch a lot of ballet.'

'Without having to perform?' Nikolai offered.

'Yes.' Rachel nodded.

'You could publish your reviews.'

He took the tiny whisper of her dream and breathed

life into it but she could see only the pitfalls. 'That's what I'd like to do but who'd read it?'

'Anya would.' Nikolai smirked. 'She would have an alert on her own name, I can assure you.'

'I've set up a blog,' Rachel admitted. 'I just haven't done anything with it but I was thinking, maybe people would one day subscribe or if there were links… It's probably a stupid idea.'

'It's not a stupid idea at all,' Nikolai refuted. 'You would know ballet better than most arts journalists.' He thought about it for a long moment. 'There are different ways to make a living now. Sev's success with Internet security could not have been dreamt of until recently. Perhaps you could speak with him, maybe he can give you some pointers.'

Rachel laughed at the very idea. 'I think he deals with far bigger fish. I'm barely a tadpole…'

'Sev knows how these things work. He would help you I am sure.'

'Will you ask him?'

'It's his wedding night.'

'Not now,' Rachel said. 'Another time.'

'I think you need to speak with Libby about that.'

He was letting her know again that he would not be sticking around.

'I need to think about it,' Rachel said. 'I don't have to rush into anything.'

'Sometimes it is better to rush,' Nikolai said. 'Or we can find ourselves in the same place convinced that we have no choice but to stay where we are.'

'I guess.'

She glanced over at Sev and tried to imagine asking Libby if she could arrange for her to speak with him.

In fact, Rachel imagined trying to ask anybody for help.

She was fiercely independent in all that she did and had got used to relying on no one—she had found that it hurt too much to be let down.

'Come on,' Nikolai said as he stood.

No, he didn't need to ask if she wanted to dance.

He took her hand and she felt his warm, dry fingers close around hers as he led her onto the dance floor.

There, her hands went to his neck as if at her own whim this time, and his moved to her waist, but instead of holding her away he pulled her in close.

His body against hers felt sublime—muscled and strong, he held her in a different way from what she was used to, for there was nothing she needed to do. Nikolai's jaw was scratching her cheek as his mouth found her ear. 'Can you hear me?' he asked.

'No,' Rachel lied, because his deep voice tickled her ear and his breath was warm, but she smiled as he moved in and held her tighter against him.

'Can you hear me now?' he checked.

'A little.'

And so he moved in closer still.

How lovely he was to dance with, Rachel thought.

There was a very calm presence to him, a certain confidence in the way he held her, and there were no words needed, just the sway of their bodies and the slow burn of desire with the quiet certainty they would end the night in bed.

Bad Rachel, she thought.

Only she didn't feel bad in his arms.

She had, with André, even if their relationship had been a casual one, always been faithful. Rachel did not do relationships well but the ending of that one had stung.

More than that, news of his marriage had caused a sense of panic that her dance world and now her family were about to collide.

Dance was where she went to escape. It was where she could be provocative and sexy, all without judgement.

There was no judgement in Nikolai's arms.

That was how she felt.

His cologne might just as well have been designed with her in mind, for the complex scent made her reel and want to bury her face in his neck and then caress his ear with her mouth.

'You dance well,' she said, and pulled her head back.

'With a good partner, you can't not,' Nikolai said.

Yes, they were talking about what was to come.

And so they danced and, for Nikolai, it was a refuge. He could feel Sev looking over at times. Clearly he wanted a proper conversation but that would not be possible tonight.

'You know you're not allowed out of my sight.' Rachel's lips stretched into a smile as their foreheads met.

'So I've heard.'

A slow dance had never felt more delicious. He moved with her and their lips ached to meet. It felt as if there were only the two of them present and then it became imperative that that be the case.

'Where are you staying tonight?' Rachel asked.

'I haven't booked anywhere yet.'

He did think of taking her back to his yacht, but that would reveal more information about himself than he wanted to give.

'It's lucky I've got a suite, then,' Rachel said.

She was bold, Nikolai thought, and he liked it. She didn't play coy and she didn't play games.

'I want your mouth,' he told her, because he was over words and now wanted to taste.

'I know you do,' Rachel said, and they could not kiss here for both knew they would be unable to stop. It was her mouth that now came to his ear and she told him the number of her suite. Her words came out breathless for his hands moved up from her hips and past her waist. They came to rest just a touch lower than she would have liked for he made her breasts ache in anticipation with that seductive motion. It was a telling touch—his palms were warm and a heady combination of firm and subtle and spoke of their mutual desire.

'Go,' he told her.

Rachel didn't go, though, because his cheek dragged against hers and he found her mouth and made her dizzy with a light but lingering kiss. There was a small potent taste that was transferred and embedded and made her lick her lips for more as he pulled his mouth back.

'Go,' he said again, now that her body smouldered.

He watched as she did so, saw how she pulled that dress down over her thighs.

She opened up her bag and checked her phone and he watched as her hair tumbled forward, then she glanced back at him as if to make sure he would follow.

They shared a look just as Rachel left and, after a suitable pause, Nikolai would leave too.

He had seen his friend marry, he had been to the reception, now he could leave. But the groom had other ideas and caught him just as he headed off.

'You're leaving?' Sev checked.

'I am.' Nikolai nodded. 'It was good to see you again. To know that you are happy.'

'Nikolai, when can we speak properly? I head off in the morning for my honeymoon but—'

'I am going overseas tomorrow or the day after,' Nikolai answered, hoping that that would be that. He could not bear the thought of an inquisition but it would seem Sev was not prepared to lose his friend again.

'Then I shall delay the honeymoon and meet with you tomorrow.'

'You wouldn't do that to your new bride,' Nikolai said, but then stiffened when Sev gestured for Naomi to join them.

'Naomi,' he said, 'Nikolai has to head overseas today or tomorrow.'

'Then we can put off the honeymoon—you two need to catch up. I know how important it is.' Naomi smiled at Nikolai.

He did not return it.

'Nikolai.' Sev spoke now. 'I didn't look for you because I thought you had died. Had I known—'

'When do you get back from your honeymoon?' Nikolai interrupted—he did not want to upset the lovely mood of the night, neither did he want to speak of that time with Naomi present.

'In two weeks' time,' Sev answered.

'I'll stay till then,' Nikolai agreed.

'You're sure?'

Nikolai nodded and Sev shook his hand.

'It will be good to catch up properly,' Sev said.

Nikolai doubted that it would be. Right now Sev could look him in the eyes and there was no awkward pause or embarrassment from his friend. He doubted it would be the case once Sev found out more about the past.

Yet he gave Sev his word that he would stay around. In fact, he gave him his cell phone number.

'I'll pass it on to Daniil,' Sev said.

They were back in touch.

Nikolai offered congratulations again and then headed out of the ballroom. He glanced at the elevators and changed his mind about heading up to Rachel's suite. Everything was gathering in and it felt too close. The temptation was to simply leave. He even pictured tossing his phone in the Thames, just deleting that line of contact rather than have them find out what had taken place.

Yet as he headed out of the hotel and walked down the red carpet he remembered standing there with Rachel and her dancing to a tune that did not exist.

He ran his tongue over his lips and recalled the taste of her flesh and the oil of her lipstick and thought of the slight gap to her teeth and her smile. From sharing the order of service with him to insisting he come to the reception and fudging the table plan, her presence had made a supremely difficult day pleasant.

Nikolai thought of her waiting for him, and he thought of his desire and he did not think of the consequences.

As he headed back into the hotel Rachel was all that was on his mind.

CHAPTER FOUR

HE WAS TAKING AGES.

She turned on every light, and with reason—Rachel was petrified of the dark, not that anyone knew. She would make sure the bedroom door stayed open—if he turned off the bedside light he might not bother to get up and turn out the lounge light.

It was a familiar black game.

She could not sleep next to anybody else and would force herself to stay awake.

No wonder her relationships never survived.

Yet she had never felt comfortable enough with anyone to tell them of her fear of the dark, let alone all the other stuff that had happened in her life.

Not even Libby.

Rachel heard his footsteps in the corridor and did not wait for a knock at the door.

Instead, she felt giddy relief as she opened it and he stepped in to her smile.

He liked it that she did not offer small talk, or a drink, that instead she took her hands and placed them around his neck and she was back on eye level with him.

'You,' Rachel said, 'were a very unexpected surprise today.'

'As were you.' She really had been, Nikolai thought. Had he known that he would be recognised and that the entire congregation would turn their focus on him he would never have gone. As for staying for the reception—he would not have considered it, had it not been for Rachel. Today had not gone as planned in the least but it had certainly been made better by having her at his side.

Now she stood in front of him. Her hands moved to his tie and unknotted it, and he felt it slide around his neck as she removed it.

He stared at her mouth and then kissed her as he had wanted to on the dance floor.

Such a kiss. He just claimed her mouth and his jaw was rough, his tongue hot and probing. It was a kiss that made her moan into his mouth and press herself into him.

His hands moved down the velvet of her dress and he felt her toned buttocks and dug in his fingers.

She could feel the press of his large hands and she ached for him to lift her up.

She kissed from the groin, Nikolai thought.

Usually so too did he.

All afternoon and into the night he had watched her smooth down the skirt of her dress and now he hitched it up and Rachel pressed in harder. She moaned in his mouth as he slid her panties down and she stepped out of them. Her hand went into his jacket.

Straight to sex, Nikolai thought, and that was usually the way he liked it, yet he wanted to explore that mouth some more, he wanted to see and to feel the body that had had him on slow burn all afternoon. And so, instead of kissing her harder, instead of peeling off her dress or lifting her, Nikolai shrugged his jacket to the floor and kissed her more slowly.

He held her cheeks and took her mouth, again and again, in sensual bites, tasting and then removing his lips as his hands caressed his face. It was a more intimate kiss than she had ever known and he refused to be rushed.

He moved from her mouth to her cheek and then down the slide of her pale slender neck where the same teasing resumed—the soft beat of his mouth, the wetness of his tongue and then the coolness of air as his mouth hovered over the next patch of skin that would know this bliss.

They should be almost done by now, Rachel thought. She should have her legs wrapped around him and her back to the wall, yet he demanded more from them and for a moment she succumbed.

Her head went back, just to allow better access to his mouth, his hand slid in her hair and she let her head be held by his palm.

Her eyes closed in bliss as his lips parted on her skin and his tongue found a beating pulse and stroked it. Then he removed his mouth and, still holding the weight of her head in his palm, he met her gaze.

She almost folded over at the lust she saw there.

Her head dropped back a fraction as he removed his hand, and then, without a word, he led her from the lounge to the bedroom.

Rachel's legs were shaking. She felt wobbly as if wearing heels for the first time. Her mouth was wet and her neck too. She went to undress, but he did not allow it; instead he kissed her down onto the bed. But Rachel only ever did things her way. She loathed the thought of a man on top so she moved from under him and knelt up.

Nikolai leant back against the pillows and refused to be rushed.

She went to take off her dress but was halted by three words. 'I undress you.'

Rachel wasn't accustomed to such a delay in proceeding and sat there a little unsure as he undid his shirt and exposed his torso. He kicked off his shoes and socks and her breath seemed to trip her up as he slid off his belt and undid his zipper and then stopped.

'Come here,' he said, and he sat up as his eyes told her she would be kissed again.

And she wanted his kiss.

Again.

Rachel chose to indulge him.

She sat on his thighs so her head was higher than his. He lifted her dress and positioned her so she could feel his erection against her naked sex.

He got back to her neck and this time her hands were the ones holding his head, knotting her fingers in his thick hair and giving into the pleasure of his deep slow kiss as her sex ached to be filled.

He sat up a little so that his head was on the headrest and the pillows supported his shoulders. Now she wanted more of this slow kiss and it was her mouth that chased him.

He lay, kissing her back, still slowly, as she moved her body provocatively over his, with only their mouths touching.

He demanded her tongue and suckled it and then when she offered hers he stroked the outside of her thighs as he kissed her deep.

Now she had to taste him, not his mouth but his skin. Nikolai's shirt was open and she slid down his body and took her time to run her fingers over his wide chest and down his strong arms. She revelled in the feel of his skin and then she tasted. Salty, delicious, she took her time to relish him, offering tiny teasing bites followed by deep sucks to his nipples.

His moan as she moved down told her he was struggling now to be patient. His erection was huge and she lingered to feel him as she stripped him of his bottom half.

Warm and hard, she could not not hold him.

His hand moved to push hers away because he loathed being touched like that.

Usually.

Except he watched the pale hand that had held the order of service, her slender fingers, the coral nail varnish on her nails, and he gave a low curse in Russian—it was not an order to stop.

He watched as her fingers moistened as she built him to near climax.

She could feel his eyes on her hand and they both watched her work and then she halted. She licked her lips and went to lower her head. She wanted to taste him but she was selfish enough to want him inside her so she changed her mind.

'Tease...' he said.

'Am I?' She smiled and so too did he.

Neither usually smiled during sex—it was necessary rather than intimate—but tonight they did.

Again she went to take off her dress, just to be naked with him, but he shook his head and said it again. 'I undress you.'

'Undress me, then.' It came out like a plea but he ignored it and she watched with her top teeth biting her lip as he slid a condom on.

'Come here.'

He positioned her over him but even then he took his time. He saw the fire of her sex. It burned brighter than her hair and she shivered as his fingers stroked and explored her. He lowered her down onto him and she let out a moan as he stretched and filled her.

And even as she positioned herself he held her and as she started to move, still he reached for her and demanded her kiss.

He dizzied her. The way he moaned at the pleasure of her rather than demand that she slow down.

The way between deep kisses he looked down and let out another moan as he watched.

Rachel raised herself up and put her hands on his chest and moved faster.

She always called the shots in bed.

But this was no 'poor boy' who couldn't deal with that.

She used him and he let her, but he could be patient when he so chose.

He was heavenly, Rachel thought. She looked down but not at his eyes. She loved the sight of his torso and she loved how his hand held her buttocks but did not guide her. She knew he watched as she closed her eyes and her lips parted, and she knew he must be about to come from the sounds that he made. His hands now took control and he moved her buttocks and guided her to a slower pace and it felt divine to rest her mouth on his as he did.

Her thighs started to tremble and she felt the familiar

rush of electricity streak down her spine as she came to him. She let out a sob.

Feeling the grip of intimate muscle, the tight shiver of her body, it took all Nikolai had in him to hold back. Instead, he just moved her slowly over his length until the fire in her slowly died.

Breathless, she knelt, resting her forehead on him, waiting for the sickly trickle of guilt to arrive, and it took her a moment to realise he hadn't come.

She met his eyes briefly and then there was a slight flurry of panic as she was plunged into darkness as he slid her dress over her head.

She was still coming down from her orgasm as he unhooked her bra and then he lifted her from him. He rolled them and she found herself on her back but resisted when he came over her. Nikolai read the small tussle and instead he lay on his side.

Rachel did not face him.

She lay staring at the ceiling, feeling him turned on beside her and planning how he would take her.

She wanted it over, yet her body thrummed in anticipation. He lifted her legs so they came over his thighs and he hooked into her and took her side on.

Rachel had never had sex like this. She was on her back but not beneath him, just exposed to his hands.

One hand roamed her breasts and stomach as he took her. The other was under her neck, his fingers in her hair as he kissed her ear.

She started to arch and his hand on her stomach pressed her down as he drove into her.

It was bliss, to be taken but not crushed, to be so relentlessly kissed and explored.

Now his finger probed her clitoris and her thighs started to ache and Nikolai moved faster.

He said something in Russian and as he moved harder within even her chin seemed to shiver.

His large hand moved to her inner thigh and held her wide open as he drove in, yet his mouth on the side of her neck was soft and sensual.

'This...' Rachel said, even if it made no sense, but she lay there arching as she felt the delicious final swell of him. And she shouted it again as she started to come, but it was from the inside this time. It was a deep drag and tightening that made her hand move down to hold herself from the onslaught. He gave her no escape or pause, though. Nikolai shot into her, over and over, his head pressed into hers, his hand over hers, where she held her sex. And they both lay there as they faded. More confusing for Rachel was that he kissed her down from a place she had never been.

She glimpsed tenderness she had never known and just for a moment she glimpsed something else—a couple in bed, both breathless, both sated.

And no shame.

The air now felt cool and Nikolai kicked down the bedding and then pulled it over them. Now came the part that Rachel dreaded—Nikolai turned off his bedside light and then stretched over her body to do the same on her side.

'Leave it on,' Rachel said.

'It's too bright.'

His response was not dismissive, it was natural, normal and adult.

The light was switched off and the room plunged into darkness save the beam of light from the lounge area.

Rachel didn't know how to share the fact that she was terrified of the dark. It would only lead to more questions. And how could she tell Nikolai that she dared not go to sleep with a man beside her? Rachel could feel his hand gently roaming her body but, as nice as it felt now, if he did that while she was asleep, it might jolt her awake with a scream.

The oddest thing for her was that, for the first time in her life, she almost felt as if she could tell him. He was such a calm and assured person and she also knew a little of his past. But that wasn't what tonight was about. He had already told her he would be on his way soon. It was better just to pretend to be asleep and to make it through the night. She could feel that Nikolai was awake beside her.

Their lovemaking had left her sated and exhausted and she had to fight not to close her eyes and give in to the sleep that beckoned her.

He could feel her awake beside him and he got up and went through to the lounge. He was about to turn out the light when he saw his jacket on the floor and the store label seemed to taunt him as he remembered the plans he had made to get through the wedding unnoticed.

Now he had promised to stay until Sev returned from his honeymoon. He knew that soon the questions would start and the truth would come out.

The past had finally caught up with him and he wanted it back where it belonged.

And then another stinging thought occurred—she would find out too. Today and tonight had been amazing and soon it would be spoiled when she discovered the truth.

He had never had to deal with this—a lover knowing.

And what a lover.

It would be bad enough telling his friends and seeing the distaste in their eyes and answering difficult questions.

But Rachel?

Yuri would say he was running from things, hiding things, and that wasn't Nikolai's way at all.

Yet at four in the morning he went into the bedroom and picked his clothes up from the floor and dressed.

'Rachel...' His voice was not as measured as he preferred, instead he had to clear his throat, but she lay there pretending, Nikolai was sure, to be asleep.

He didn't say her name again—he just collected his belongings and was gone.

As the door closed behind him he was almost tempted to knock, and say what? That he'd locked himself out or...?

No, better she thought him a bastard than for the truth to come out, he thought as he stepped out onto dark London streets.

Nikolai had thought he had long ago dealt with his past.

It would seem he had been wrong.

CHAPTER FIVE

RACHEL HEARD THE door close behind him and rolled to her side and turned on the side light.

Bastard!

She lay back on the pillow, telling herself that she shouldn't have expected anything more from him. It had been just about sex after all. And yet, when he had held her hips and slowed her down, when he had silently insisted on eye contact she had felt connection. It had been the first time she had almost trusted her body to another. She had handed herself over to him and she had glimpsed how it felt to let go and relax into another's embrace.

Now she felt hollow and empty and ashamed of herself.

She tried not to beat herself up about it—told herself that there had been no one, apart from André, for years, but Nikolai's silent departure cheapened what had taken place.

It was a restless sleep that followed and Rachel woke to the bleep of her phone and read the text.

A girl!

There was a photo attachment and Rachel looked at

a huge white blanket with just a tiny red face peeking out. *She* was finally here.

So beautiful! Congratulations!!! Does she have a name?

Rachel texted her message and then awaited the response.

Not yet.

As Rachel texted to say that she would be in this afternoon at visiting time she was surprised to find that she was crying. They were happy tears, she told herself, except it didn't feel like they were. She was happy for her friend and thrilled that the baby had arrived safely, yet lying alone in the vast bed, missing a man she had only just met, served to expose the mess of her own life.

And it was a mess, she thought.

A hot mess and there was no escaping that fact.

She had just walked out on her career without much thought for the future and now she'd had a one-night stand with a man who came and went—literally.

Rachel had seen a psychologist once in an effort to address her murky past and she hadn't liked what she had heard—women with histories similar to hers tended to go one of two ways, she had been told. They were either mistrusting of men or promiscuous.

This morning Rachel felt as if she had achieved both.

So instead of using her late check-out and languishing with breakfast in bed, Rachel stuffed her hair into a cap. The tears that had started kept flowing. It had been such a long time since she'd cried and tears were only ever shed in private.

Even as she got dressed and packed up her overnight bag the tears would not stop. Then, as she did a final sweep of the room, there, under the chair where he had taken off his jacket, were his sunglasses.

They were a saving grace because at least she could cover her eyes as she checked out, but tears kept trickling from beneath them.

Damn Nikolai!

Why had he had to kiss her like that? Why had he had to look deep into her eyes and demand more from her than she usually gave?

It felt like the stopper had been pulled on her emotions, Rachel thought as she took the Underground home. Every feeling she kept so carefully hidden, every emotion that she guarded seemed to have been shaken loose by last night. It wasn't just him, Rachel told herself as she stepped into the house. It was her career, it was her cousin's wedding and also seeing Libby a mother.

Something that would surely never happen to her.

She couldn't even manage a successful relationship let alone imagine raising a child. Anyway, wasn't it children who were scared of the dark?

Not their mother.

Home provided little solace. Once she had lived for lazy Sundays when there had been no performance to prepare for, no class or practice. It had been the one day when her body could recover from the rigours of the week, a day when she could lie in bed and catch up on some sleep.

This Sunday, though, was spent trying to soothe her swollen eyelids with tea bags and then getting ready to go and visit Libby. Rachel had to somehow prepare to be her usual bright, bubbly self.

She erased her freckles with that amazing foundation, though it didn't work its necessary magic with the tip of her red nose. She did what she could to play down her swollen eyes and then added a double dose of coral lipstick. She chose to wear her favourite willow-green wraparound dress. Initially she tried it with nude flats then changed her mind and opted for heels instead, just to bolster her confidence.

She pushed out a smile in the mirror and saw the horrible gap in her front teeth.

Tomorrow she *was* going to make an appointment for braces, Rachel decided and then recalled Nikolai's words. *'Why would you ruin such an amazing mouth?'*

She recalled their long, slow flirtation and how easy he had been to talk to. How she'd told him about her idea for a blog and he hadn't laughed. Instead, he had made suggestions.

Rachel wished, how she wished, he hadn't been so good.

She stopped at the hospital gift shop and bought a large bunch of flowers along with a little pink balloon. She would buy the baby a proper present this week but for now she headed through the corridors of the private hospital towards the maternity wing. As she entered Rachel stiffened when she saw that André was speaking with the receptionist. He turned as she made her way over and shook his head.

'Libby's not taking any visitors,' he said to Rachel.

'Oh!' Rachel looked at the receptionist. 'Is everything okay?'

'I believe everything's fine. I've just got her marked here as not to be disturbed.'

Rachel stood for an uncomfortable second, wondering if she should explain that they were very close friends but not sure of the difference that might make. Then she understood the visitor ban as she glanced down the corridor and saw some of her troupe heading in. Poor Libby! It was Sunday so every dancer who knew her would be squeezing a visit in today.

'Could you pass these on to her?' Rachel said, and handed over the flowers.

'Of course.'

She turned to go but André caught up. 'Hey, wait,' he called, and Rachel wished she could put up a little 'do not disturb' sign of her own.

Very deliberately she stopped her shoulders from stiffening and forced a smile before turning around.

'I just heard the news that you've left.' André made his way over to her. 'I'm shocked. We all are. You gave no hint—'

'When would I have, André?' Rachel asked. 'During one of our deep and meaningful conversations? Oh, that's right, we never had them.'

'You're upset about Shona…'

'No.' Rachel shook her head.

Yes, she was.

But not for the reasons he thought—André had merged her worlds and she loathed that he had.

'You are,' he insisted. 'I never took you as being jealous…'

'I'm not jealous, André,' she corrected him sharply. 'But really—my cousin? Don't you think that's a bit off?'

'For God's sake!' André protested. 'You're being ridiculous.'

Rachel wasn't going to stand there and debate it but

the truth was, the thought that he was marrying her cousin made her skin crawl. Now, at every family gathering, every wedding or christening she would have to see him, her ex-lover. The fact that he didn't see it as a problem infuriated her. So much so that she walked off briskly and left him to catch up with the rest of their troupe.

Or rather what had once been her troupe.

She wasn't a part of that world any more. Now she had told Libby and the word was out, it was truly starting to dawn on her that her dancing career, as she had known it, was over.

And, because it really wasn't a great Sunday, coming towards her in the corridor was last night's mistake, naturally.

Nikolai.

What the hell was he doing here? Rachel thought. He was the last person she'd expected to see, given how keen he'd been to get away after the wedding service.

Unfortunately for her he looked amazing. If he'd looked beautiful yesterday, he looked exquisite now. Dressed in black linen pants with a fitted shirt, Nikolai could have been strolling down a runway in Milan. He hadn't shaved and looked sulky and beautiful and he too was carrying flowers.

'Rachel,' he said as she passed him.

He had seen her talking to an exceptionally goodlooking man and then had watched her flounce off in a huff.

It was André. He knew that, he could just tell that they had been lovers.

They had stood closer than friends would have, their

body language had told him they were sexually familiar with each other and it did not sit well with him.

Jealousy was not an emotion that Nikolai was used to feeling, yet he had felt it surge as he had turned the corner and seen them. Still, it wasn't his place to be jealous, he knew, but as she brushed past him he caught her elbow and said her name.

'What?' she asked as she swung around.

Nikolai took in her red eyes and swollen lips and though he wasn't sure if he had been the cause of her tears he knew that his leaving had been less than kind.

'About last night…'

'You lost your opportunity for conversation about four a.m. this morning,' she said, her voice tart.

'Look—'

'I don't want to look,' she broke in swiftly. She did *not* want to examine last night and this morning's tears; she did *not* want to remember the summer bliss of his arms and the cold winter of this morning. She glanced down at the flowers he held. 'You really shouldn't have,' Rachel said in a sarcastic tone.

'I don't think pink is your colour,' he responded. 'In fact, I doubt that flowers are even your thing.'

That he was right almost brought a reluctant smile to her lips but Rachel refused to let it appear.

'They're for Libby,' he said.

'Well, Libby's not accepting visitors.'

'Good.'

His response confused her but Rachel wasn't waiting around to find out what he'd meant by that. As Nikolai went to hand them over to the receptionist, she made her way to the elevator.

Please, hurry, she thought, pressing the button over and over, but luck wasn't on her side today.

Oh, no!

The day just got better and better because first André and then Nikolai came and stood by her side and she had the absolute displeasure of getting into the elevator with both men.

'I hear they're having drinks for you on Saturday afternoon,' André said. Of course he was oblivious to the other man in the lift, whereas Rachel was acutely aware of him.

'No.' Rachel shook her head. 'I couldn't make it then, so it's been moved to the Saturday after.'

She had deliberately moved her leaving do to the following Saturday afternoon in the hope that, given that the next day was his wedding, André wouldn't be able to make it.

'Rachel…' André said as the elevator doors opened and she started to leave. 'Let's go and get a drink and discuss—'

'She can't.'

It was Nikolai who broke in.

André frowned at the intrusion but then Rachel tensed as Nikolai spoke on. 'Rachel and I were just on our way out.'

CHAPTER SIX

'YOU DIDN'T NEED to do that.' Rachel said.

André had huffed off and now Rachel stood awkwardly in the hospital reception with the man who had so coldly left her in bed earlier that morning.

'Do what?' Nikolai said.

'Make up excuses for me.'

'I'm not making up an excuse,' he said. 'We *are* on our way out.'

Rachel angrily shook her head. 'Oh, no, we're not.' She went to walk off.

'Don't rush off.'

She spun around and faced him. 'I could have said the same last night.'

He smiled at her sharp response and, for Rachel, the effect was just as dazzling as it had been yesterday. It was rare, she knew, for she hadn't even seen him smile with his friends. It was almost her undoing but not quite.

'Come on.' He sensed a tiny dint in her armour and moved straight in. 'I want to apologise properly for my behaviour this morning.'

Momentarily, the wind was taken from Rachel's angry sails, though it swiftly returned. 'Had we not bumped into each other you wouldn't have—'

'Rachel.' He was calm as he interrupted her tirade. 'I accept that you don't know me very well but I think even you could agree that a hospital visit to a woman I don't know, a few hours after she has given birth, is not the norm for me. I only came because I was going to ask Libby or Daniil for your number and I thought it better to do that face to face,' Nikolai admitted.

'I don't believe you.'

'Whether you do or not is up to you.' Nikolai shrugged.

'And what were you going to do if Libby gave it to you?'

'The same as I am doing now—ask if you want to go and get dinner so I can better explain my actions.'

'So,' Nikolai pushed. 'Shall we go and get something to eat?'

'It's four o'clock,' Rachel pointed out.

'Well, I'm hungry.'

So was she. Not just for food, though.

'Fine.'

It was against every rule she made for herself. Usually she would leave and insist on a more thorough pursuit, yet she was painfully aware that there was a ticking clock attached to Nikolai—he would be leaving soon. She wanted to know him some more, and that he had apologised up front for his behaviour had taken her by surprise.

Nikolai had felt bad all day and that was something that didn't happen often. Yesterday had been difficult.

Today was proving to be the same.

'We can walk or get a taxi,' Nikolai offered. 'It's close by.'

'What is?'

'The place I want to take you—a bar I know.' What

he didn't tell her was that the Russian vodka piano bar was one of several that he owned around the world. Instead, he glanced down at her pale legs and high heels and made the choice for them. 'Taxi.'

Soon he had hailed one and they climbed in, Nikolai gave the address and then turned and saw her strained face as she looked out of the window.

'I assume that the man in the elevator was your ex.'

'Does it matter?' she answered—after Nikolai's behaviour she certainly didn't have to explain herself to him.

It mattered to Nikolai.

On sight he had decided that he didn't like André. It wasn't just the stir of jealousy that had hit him when he had seen Rachel talking to the other man in the corridor, more he did not like a man who suggested drinks with an ex two weeks before his wedding.

There was something about Rachel that concerned him—or rather there was a vulnerability to her, despite her confident exterior, and he had no doubt in his mind that a man like André might use that to his own advantage.

Her phone rang and seeing it was Libby she took it.

'I just got your flowers,' Libby moaned. 'Why didn't you give your name? You were on the list of people allowed in to visit.'

'André was standing next to me,' Rachel said. 'And then another half a dozen arrived. You get some sleep, I'll see you when you get home.'

'Nikolai came to visit too and left flowers,' Libby said. 'I feel awful for abandoning him last night…'

'You hardly had a choice,' Rachel said, and looked at him. 'I'm sure he was fine.' They chatted for a couple of moments but Rachel chose not to mention she was in a taxi with Nikolai.

'How is she?' he asked when she finished the call.

'A bit teary,' Rachel said. 'She was even worried about abandoning you last night.'

'I'm an orphan,' he said. 'So I'm kind of used to it.'

His dark, dry humour made her smile, just a little, and he made her so curious that for a moment she forgot how cross she was. 'Do you know who your parents were?'

Her direct question surprised Nikolai, or maybe not—this was Rachel after all. He answered with a brief shake of his head.

'Not at all?' she asked.

'No.' He met her eyes and chose to end the conversation. 'I was left in a box in the church.'

Or rather it should have ended the conversation but Rachel chimed in again. 'How old were you then?'

'A day or so old.'

He looked out of the window, loathing the discomfort that admission caused—but at least he had silenced her. After all, what could anyone say to that? he thought to himself.

'That was nice of her.' Rachel's voice broke into his thoughts.

He frowned and then turned and looked at her. 'Nice?'

'For your mother to leave you where she must have known you'd be found.'

He got back to looking out of the window, not that that stopped Rachel from talking.

'Poor thing.'

'I don't need your sympathy,' he snapped.

'I meant your mum.' Rachel tapped at his leg with her foot and he looked up and she was smiling her toothy smile because he had misunderstood and Nikolai found himself almost smiling back.

'Why do you think that?'

'Well, from the sound of things Libby is struggling a bit today and she's got Daniil and all the nurses helping her...and I can't imagine how awful it must be to feel you have no choice other than to give your baby up.'

Nikolai hadn't thought of it like that, he had never thought it might have been hard for his mother to do what she had. 'Do you want children?' he asked.

'No,' Rachel said. 'I'm far too selfish.'

She wasn't selfish, though, Nikolai thought. She was very, very kind because in her rather direct way she had turned things around a little for him, and, no, she wasn't glib, she was blunt but kind.

'Anyway, I'm not talking to you.' Rachel remembered then she was supposed to be cross and got back to sulking, but the taxi was pulling up and they were soon getting out.

The street was quiet and there was no restaurant that Rachel could see, at first anyway.

'This way.'

It was a place you wouldn't go to unless you knew that it was here, Rachel thought, because they walked down some steps into a basement and the door was opened for them.

Nikolai spoke in Russian to the *maître d'* and told him that he didn't want any extra fuss to be made of him and his guest.

They were used to his request—but as they were led through the bar it dawned on Nikolai that Rachel, unlike any other of the women that he dated, had absolutely no idea about his wealth. He had dressed down for the wedding and had used taxis rather than his driver in an effort to keep his life from his friends—to hide his identity somewhat—but there was less and less need for that now. Soon he would be speaking with Sev and it would all come out. Nikolai had decided to face things. He would rather that Rachel heard the sparse details he was prepared to share from him than from anyone else.

And if she had questions, he would do his best to answer them.

The bar was semi-dark, the tables lit by candles, and a piano played in the background. As they took their seats at low velvet couches it was slightly disorientating—there were no clocks, the lights were dimmed, it could be midnight or midday.

'Wow!' Rachel said as they sat down. Her eyes had become accustomed to the gloom and she took in her surroundings—the clientele was exquisitely dressed. There was an air of both opulence and decadence. 'So this is where all the beautiful people disappear to on a Sunday.'

'It is,' Nikolai said as they were handed some menus.

Rachel peered at the extensive list and shook her head. 'I have no idea what I want,' she admitted. 'It all looks...' she thought for a moment '...unfamiliar.'

'Then I shall order for you,' he said.

'Please.'

He thought she might have protested but Rachel was actually thrilled to just sit back on the sofa as he gave the waitress their order in Russian.

'What am I getting?' she asked.

'You will find out soon.'

'So—' she got straight to the point '—you wanted to apologise.'

'Can we at least eat first?'

Two shot glasses and a bottle were brought over and Nikolai poured. It felt rather debauched to be sipping icy vodka that burnt her tongue this early in the afternoon.

'What do you taste?' Nikolai asked.

'Ginger...' She rolled her tongue over her lips just to taste it again. 'It's amazing.'

'It is actually my favourite,' he said. 'It was so, even before I saw your hair.'

Rachel put down her glass and shot him a look. 'Don't try flirting, Nikolai,' she warned. 'I'm still cross with you.'

'I know that you are, and I will deal with that soon, but first it's time to eat.'

He poured her another drink and as the food was brought over for them to share he talked her through it. It was hard to remember to stay cross as delight after delight passed her lips. Tiny *pirozhkis*, which Nikolai explained were small pies but crammed with amazing ingredients, like wild mushrooms and smoked meats.

There were little blinis topped with caviar, which was her favourite thing. Furthermore, there wasn't just a small smattering. These were absolutely loaded and Rachel closed her eyes in utter bliss as the caviar popped in her mouth and then she caught him looking.

'If you're trying to win favour with food,' she said, 'then you're doing a very good job.'

'You like caviar?'

'I love it,' she admitted. 'I could very happily eat it for breakfast every day.'

It wasn't just the caviar that was wonderful—who

knew cabbage could be sexy? But when it was red and dressed in a ginger relish to go with their drink of choice, Rachel could feel her cheeks grow warm.

'That's amazing,' she admitted.

'So are you.'

She gave a short, wry laugh and remembered the reason they were there. 'Clearly not that amazing,' she said, and then her eyes darted angrily at him.

'Say what you are thinking,' he invited.

'That you're a bastard!'

'I often am,' he freely admitted. 'But not in this case.'

'Oh, I beg to differ.' She let out a terse breath. Even though it was refreshing to discuss issues it was still a difficult conversation to have—it was hard to admit how hurt she was by his actions because that meant she liked him and that was not something she ever cared to admit.

'I regret how I left this morning,' he said. 'Usually I don't dwell on mistakes. All day, though, I have. You didn't deserve to have me leave like that.'

'You made me feel cheap,' she said. 'I wasn't expecting you to get down on your knees and propose the next morning—I'm not naïve—but to just walk off...' She stopped talking then. She could hear the slight rise in her voice and she could feel the prickle of anger spreading over her skin. And now she knew the reason that she had shed so many tears. The way he had left her had awoken an emotional memory, one that she did not want to explore.

'I tried to tell you I was leaving,' he said, 'but you were busy pretending to be asleep.'

He was too direct even for Rachel—there were some

things you just didn't say, some things that you allowed to go unobserved.

Not Nikolai, it would seem.

'You were uncomfortable afterwards,' he continued, 'and so was I. I don't know why you were. I can only speak for myself...' Rachel sat and fiddled with her glass as he spoke on. 'It wasn't my intention to get back in touch with my friends,' he explained. 'Yesterday I planned just to go to the church. I really wanted to see Sev get married but I didn't want to have the conversation that I knew would follow if I was seen. If I catch up with them again they will have questions...'

'Of course they will,' Rachel said. 'They want to know what happened to you over the years.'

Nikolai said nothing for a moment, he just refilled his glass. He didn't mind his friends asking about the missing years; more it was the thought of them asking why he had left in the first place. Even as he spoke on, he was trying to work out how best to explain things. 'For now there hasn't been time for a proper catch-up—Sev is on his honeymoon, Daniil is busy with the baby...' He saw her slight frown.

'Don't you want to be back in touch?' Rachel asked.

'In part I do,' Nikolai admitted, and then took a breath. 'I feel I owe it to Sev as well. I never knew, till yesterday, that he thought I had killed myself. Sev will want to know why I ran away.'

She took a sip of her drink but her throat felt too tight to swallow the liquid as he continued to speak.

'I was being abused by a teacher.'

Rachel swallowed the liquid down and felt a burn in her chest—not from the drink, more the impossible subject.

She could feel the scrutiny of his gaze yet she couldn't meet his eyes.

It wasn't what had happened to Nikolai that made her feel so exquisitely uncomfortable, more her own past.

He had done something about it.

The man sitting in front of her now had had the guts to run away, whereas she had lain in the dark and pretended to be asleep.

Despite the people around them, and Nikolai opposite her, she felt as if she were living it again—the sound of her mother's boyfriend pushing open her bedroom door... That was the emotional memory he had awoken this morning—being left in the dark afterwards as the door closed.

Being used and then discarded.

No, it was not a subject she would ever discuss.

She ached to have his honesty, to be able to sit there and speak the truth, to tell him she understood.

'Sexually abused,' Nikolai clarified, and she felt sweat bead on her upper lip. There were too many people around to be having such a conversation, surely?

'You don't need to tell me this.' Her voice was strangled, her eyes flashed as she told him to back off from the subject, one she wished he had never brought up. Did she tell him she'd known anyway? That his friends had already found out?

No, Rachel decided. It wasn't her place. For herself, she could think of nothing worse than others knowing. It would be like having your diary read out loud.

'I'm just letting you know why I ran away,' he said.

'I get it.'

'And I didn't want you to find out from someone else...'

'I get it, okay?'

A waitress came back with the dessert menu and, rather than look at him, Rachel read through it. She fought for normality, to slip her mask back on, but she felt as if it had been dropped to the floor.

And then she remembered.

'You left these.' She went into her bag and pulled out his sunglasses, put them on the table.

'Thanks.'

He could feel her discomfort. He could just feel how appalled she was as her hand went up to her hair and twisted a curl.

'The liquorice ice cream looks nice,' she said, and then caught his dark gaze.

'Really?' he responded coolly.

'Actually, I'm not all that hungry, I might skip dessert.'

She would rather be anywhere else than having this conversation so she went to her bag and pulled out her purse.

'It's fine,' Nikolai said.

'At least let me get half.'

'No need,' he said, but she noted he did not get out his wallet, or call for the bill. As Rachel stood she felt as if she'd been spun around and she looked for the waitress to pay.

'The bill...'

'It's fine,' he said again. 'I own the place.'

He was through covering up and he was through too with Rachel. Oh, he'd prepared himself for discomfort and awkward questions, but to have her dismiss him, to simply reach for the menu, hurt.

It really did.

A moment later they were out on the street and she stood blinking in the light.

'Nikolai…'

She had handled that terribly.

Even now she was still red in the neck; even now the brief return to her own teenage years had her heart leaping up near her throat.

'Could we…?' she started, while knowing it was too late to retrieve things—he had hailed a taxi. And not for sharing, she guessed as he held open the door.

He handed the driver some cash…

'I can pay for my own taxi.'

'I asked you here,' he said. 'And I make sure you get home.'

Alone.

He was done.

CHAPTER SEVEN

SHE HAD BEEN horribly insensitive.

Nikolai, unaware that she already knew, had told her an incredibly difficult thing.

And she'd suggested having ice cream!

Rachel had never felt more selfish. He had bared his soul and she'd closed hers off. She wanted to apologise but she simply didn't know how.

In the end, on Wednesday she called Libby. Of course, she rang to find out how she and the baby were doing, but when she got the answering-machine for the second time, instead of leaving a message, she rang again the next day.

And the next.

'Sorry, Rachel.' Libby sounded tired. 'I've been meaning to call you but it seems that every time I go to do that, she wakes up!'

'It's fine,' Rachel said. 'How is she?'

'Gorgeous, demanding, hard work. Daniil said that she clearly takes after me!'

'No name yet?'

'Almost,' Libby said. 'We'll tell you on Saturday.'

'Saturday?'

'I'm determined for you to meet her and I've got something I need to ask you. Two things, actually.'

'Such as?' Rachel frowned.

'Can we talk on Saturday?' Libby said, and, in the background, the baby started to cry.

'Sure,' Rachel said. 'Who's going to be there?'

'Just us,' Libby said. 'Oh, Anya has said that she might drop in. We asked her and Nikolai…'

Rachel stayed silent but she could feel her fingers tightly gripping the phone.

'He hasn't got back to us. I think he was heading overseas after the wedding and it looks like he's gone. Daniil's texted him a few times but there's been no reply.'

'Oh.'

'I think Daniil just has to accept that he doesn't want to be in touch.'

'I guess.'

'Anyway,' Libby said as the baby's cries grew louder, 'I really do have to go.'

'Sure.'

Rachel sat for a long time after the call ended. She felt guilty, in part, for Nikolai's abrupt departure. Oh, he had said that he was leaving but she was sure, quite sure, that had she handled his admission better then maybe he'd have stayed around long enough to speak properly with his friends. No doubt he thought their reaction would be as uncomfortable and as stilted as hers had been.

'Damn,' she hissed.

Forget pride—on Saturday she would ask for his number. No matter how awkward it would be, she would ask Daniil if he would give it to her.

It was her apology that was required now.

* * *

Arriving at Daniil and Libby's luxurious penthouse with the gift she had bought, Rachel was looking forward to seeing the baby and also nervous at the thought of asking for Nikolai's number.

She had far more reason to be nervous than that!

As Daniil let her in and she walked through to the vast lounge, her eyes were drawn not to Libby, who sat holding a tiny baby, but to Nikolai, and she gave him a flustered, nervous smile. 'Hi.'

He didn't smile back. In fact, he didn't even return her greeting, just offered a very small nod.

Anya was there also and her greeting wasn't particularly effusive either. Rachel made her way over to Libby and gave her a kiss on the cheek, handing over the present.

'Swap!' Libby said, and held up the tiny baby for Rachel to hold.

She was so tiny and light and as she held her, Rachel surprised herself by feeling close to tears. She took a seat and gazed at the little girl. 'She's beautiful,' she said, stroking her soft cheek. She was utterly perfect and so innocent. 'I never want to let her go,' Rachel admitted.

'Then please don't.' Libby let out a tired sigh. 'She cries the second she's put down.'

'Don't we all?' Rachel said, her voice thick with emotion. Oh, she'd been excited for Libby but, seeing her daughter, holding her, feeling the wonder that this little person was really here, Rachel was so entranced that she forgot about Nikolai for a moment.

'Oh, Rachel…' Libby said, as she opened up the present. It was a small cashmere blanket in the softest of pinks. 'This is gorgeous.'

'I wanted to have her name embroidered on it but I still don't know it!'

'Nadia,' Daniil said. 'It means hope.'

Nikolai watched.

He tried not to but Rachel still fascinated him. He had seen Anya's cool perusal of the baby, and yet Rachel was moved to tears just at the sight of her.

'Now that we're all here,' Libby said, 'I can ask you. We want you to be her godmother, Rachel.'

'Me?'

'Now, I know it's a bit of a rush, but we want everyone to be there. Anya's heading off to Paris soon and I believe Nikolai is leaving once Sev and Naomi get back…' Libby turned to him.

'I leave a week on Monday,' Nikolai said.

'Well,' Libby continued, 'we've managed to organise next Sunday.'

Rachel felt her heart plummet. 'I can't make next Sunday. I've got a wedding—'

'You can miss André's wedding.' Libby easily removed that obstacle. 'Come on, Rachel, you said you didn't even want to go.'

'It's not that…'

Nikolai watched as Rachel's face paled and she looked down at the baby rather than at her friend. 'It's my cousin Shona's wedding.'

'Shona's getting married too?'

Nikolai, who felt little for anyone and wasn't particularly enamoured of Rachel, given her reaction to his difficult revelation, felt a stir of sympathy for her. He could sense her discomfort. Libby could not—she was far too busy slotting the jigsaw together.

'You mean Shona and André…' Libby's jaw dropped for a moment but then her mouth snapped closed and she made a face as if she'd bitten into a lemon.

'Didn't she come and see you perform in Singapore?' Libby checked.

'That's when they met,' Rachel said, though still she did not look up and Libby with her baby brain just waded in when usually she wouldn't have, at least not with others present. 'But you and he were still—'

'Libby!' Rachel said, and looked up and only then did Libby see her friend's anguish.

'Oh, Rachel, I'm sorry.'

It was awkward and embarrassing and there was nothing she could do except admit the grim truth.

'I didn't know they were seeing each other till a couple of weeks ago when my mum told me about the wedding,' Rachel said, and she could not bring herself to look at Nikolai. 'I'm sorry, Libby, I can't make the christening.'

The uncomfortable pause was broken by Anya.

'If you are short on people to ask, I can be godmother.'

Libby opened her mouth and closed it and Nikolai watched as even a blushing Rachel suppressed a smile at Anya's offer. And, because she was good friends with Libby, even though she was probably cross, Rachel came to her rescue.

'I'll speak to my mum about the wedding,' she offered. 'I'll see if I can work something out.'

'Well,' Anya said, 'the offer is there if you need me to step in. Right now I have to go.' She stood. 'It is closing night and I need time to prepare.' She glanced over at Nikolai. 'You are too late for tickets. You will have to come to Paris when you want to see me perform.'

Anya barely glanced at Rachel or even Libby and the baby as Daniil saw her out.

To break the tense silence, Libby teased Nikolai. 'Was that Anya's attempt to flirt with you?'

'No.' Nikolai shook his head. 'That's the arrogance of Anya. She was like it as a child—assuming that, of course, we all want to see her perform!'

'I do,' Rachel sighed.

She tried to push past the awkwardness of before, but really all she wanted to do was go home.

'You're not going to speak to your mum, are you?' Libby asked when Daniil had come back in and the conversation turned again to the christening.

'No, I was just saying that to give you time to come up with someone other than Anya.'

'But I want you to be there.'

'I know you do.' Rachel sighed because she badly wanted to be there too. 'My mum and aunt are very close. Shona and I played together all the time, growing up. It would look terrible if I didn't go to the wedding.'

No matter the cost to her, Nikolai thought.

'Could you do both?' Nikolai asked, surprised that he was getting involved.

'The christening's at eleven,' Libby said, and Rachel shook her head.

'The wedding's at one and it's miles away...' She tried to change the subject. 'You had two things to ask me,' Rachel reminded her friend. She just wanted this over with now.

'Oh, yes. I've got a teacher to cover for me but she has to go to a funeral in Spain next week. Rachel, I know you don't want to teach but—'

'It's fine.' Rachel nodded. 'I can manage a week.'

'Are you sure? If not, I can always ask Maria.'

'I'll do it,' Rachel said, 'though I really do have to go now…'

Everyone in the room knew that she was lying. She just wanted to be gone.

'Of course.' Libby took little Nadia as Rachel said farewell to Daniil and gave a small nod to Nikolai. At the door Libby was nearly in tears as she apologised for what she had said earlier about André.

'It's no big deal,' Rachel said.

'Of course it is. I wasn't thinking. Not that that's any excuse. I embarrassed you.'

'You were just telling the truth,' Rachel sighed. She gave her friend a kiss and left, and Libby closed her eyes and then headed back into the lounge.

'Well, I handled that brilliantly.'

'She'll be fine,' Daniil said. 'Though we will have to think about getting someone else.'

'I'll try and talk to her again.' Libby gave a shake of her head. 'I doubt it will do any good, though; Rachel's so prickly about anything to do with her family and simply won't discuss them. I don't know why. Why can't she just say no to her mother for once?'

Nikolai found that he wanted to know that as well but he remained silent as Libby looked down at her baby.

'I'm going to feed Nadia.'

And once Libby had left, for the first time in many years it was just he and Daniil.

'How have you been?' Nikolai asked. 'How did things work out for you with your adopted family?'

'They didn't,' Daniil admitted. 'But life is good now. I have Libby and Nadia. I'm back in touch with Sev.'

'He'll be living in New York,' Nikolai pointed out.

'We're going there for New Year.'

'Shared holidays...' Nikolai's voice was a touch scathing but Daniil took no offence. It was a survival technique they had all had learned, growing up—to look with contempt at those who relied on, or grew close to, others.

'It's good to spend time with friends. And now you are back. Tell me—'

'Don't forget Anya,' Nikolai interrupted, hoping to fend off the questions.

'We try to,' Daniil said, and they both shared a smile.

'She hasn't changed.'

'I think something went on with her and Roman after I left,' Daniil said. 'Did you see anything between them?'

Nikolai thought back to the couple of years he had spent in the orphanage after Daniil had left. 'Roman went into the secure part after you'd gone. I didn't see him much and as for Anya, she came back for the holidays and still practised her dance steps and helped her mother...' He shook his head. 'I left when I was fourteen, they might have had something after that.'

And he had opened the topic of his leaving. Nikolai stood and went to stare out at the magnificent view of London—Westminster and Big Ben—that stretched out before him. 'The view is good.'

His changed all the time.

Nikolai was forever moving.

He loved his life yet it felt odd to stand in a home, to be here, talking with Daniil. He could hear the baby fussing and yet it felt peaceful. 'So, you've heard nothing at all from Roman?' Nikolai asked.

'No. I can't find him. I went back last year to try and piece things together. I've been back a few times but never got anywhere. This time, though... Do you remember Sergio, the maintenance man, who coached Roman and me in boxing?'

'Of course I remember Sergio.' Nikolai said. 'He was a good man.'

'He died a few years ago.'

There was no shocked gasp or *Oh, no!* These men were used to loss and grief and never displayed it.

Daniil told Nikolai that he had something for him and headed off but returned a few moments later with a photo.

'This is a copy, keep it.'

It was the four of them as young boys. Nikolai could remember them asking Sergio to take just one picture of the four of them.

It was the only photo he had of his childhood and Nikolai found that it was too hard to remember that time.

They had been close then, happy then, not that others believed that—the home kids had said they had nothing, yet they'd had each other.

It was only when they had been forced apart by Daniil's adoption that things had started to go wrong.

Nikolai said nothing. He looked at the photo just briefly and then put it in the inside pocket of his jacket as Daniil spoke on.

'The last time I went back I spoke to Sergio's widow.

She said that Roman had run wild after I left but she thought he had joined the military. It's been a dead end since then. I was looking for Sev and trying to find out more about what had happened to you. She told me about the letter and that you had killed yourself—that your body had been found in the river...'

Nikolai felt as if he was on his yacht during rough seas. It was as if the floor had lurched from beneath him and he had to fight to keep his face impassive as he turned around. 'She told you about the letter...' Nikolai could feel his heart racing. Before running away he had written an angry letter detailing the abuse and had put it under the office door, in the hope of sparing another child from what had happened to him.

They must have thought it a suicide note.

There were so many details he could go over about that time. He had witnessed a fight and a young man being pushed into the river. He had dropped his bag, intending to dive in, but none of that mattered at this moment, just one thing.

'Did she tell you what was in the letter?''

'About the abuse?' Daniil checked, and then nodded. 'She said that the teacher was removed...'

Daniil knew, Nikolai realised.

His friend already knew and yet he sat looking him in the eye.

'Does Sev know?'

'Of course. We have been trying to piece things together...'

'And does Libby know as well?' Nikolai asked, and Daniil nodded.

'Does Libby know what?' came Libby's voice, and Nikolai glanced up as she came to the door.

'We were just talking about the reason Nikolai ran away.'

'I hope he burns in hell for what he did to you,' Libby said, and took a seat.

And that was that.

She knew too.

Nikolai had been so dreading the revelation and now he'd found that they already knew.

And if Libby knew…

'Does anybody else know?' Nikolai asked.

'Of course not,' Daniil said, but Nikolai's eyes were on Libby, who went red.

'I might have said something to Rachel…' Libby really wasn't having the best day. 'We were flatmates at the time. She was thrilled when Sev and Daniil got back in touch…'

'It's fine,' Nikolai said, but though they carried on the conversation his mind was whirring.

Rachel had known about the abuse all along.

He remembered her now turning to him at the wedding and her forthright greeting.

'Aren't you the dead one?'

She had known his history when they'd danced, she had known when they'd talked and she had known when they'd made love.

All along she had known and she had been her outgoing, effusive self.

So why the discomfort at the conversation, why had she squirmed and fought to change the subject? At the mention of abuse Rachel had practically turned and run.

It was how he had felt when Yuri had broached the subject, it was how he had felt today when he'd thought he might have to speak about it with Daniil.

He recalled her words and the flash of her eyes and now he recognised the anger that had been in them as she'd said, 'I get it, okay?'

Libby, who she discussed so much with, had just admitted that Rachel was touchy about her family but even she didn't know why.

Nikolai thought he did.

Rachel did indeed *get it*.

She had sailed that vile ship too, Nikolai was now sure of it.

CHAPTER EIGHT

RACHEL, ONCE HOME, wanted to curl up and die of embarrassment. She lay on her bed and cringed. Not only hadn't she apologised to Nikolai, he had, thanks to Libby, found out that, till recently, she'd been sleeping with André.

Oh, she did not want to guess Nikolai's opinion of her.

She had a bath in the hope of relaxing but that had stopped working ages ago.

She peeled off her shower cap and pulled on her robe. As she headed down the hall there was a knock at the door and though she thought about not answering it, she knew she'd have been seen through the glass.

It might be her mum, she thought with a weary sigh.

Instead it was Nikolai.

'Libby forgot to give you the keys to the dance studio. I said it was no problem for me to drop them around.'

He held them out to her.

'There's also a list of lesson times.'

Rachel didn't want to hear about keys and lesson times. 'I'm sorry!' Rachel said. She just blurted out the words she had been holding in all week. 'I was a cow when you told me—'

'It's fine.'

'No, no, it isn't. I was going to ask Daniil for your number but then you were there.'

He granted her the smile she'd thought she would never see again but she couldn't return it.

'I'm so embarrassed,' she admitted.

'Why?' Nikolai asked.

'Because of...' She glanced over his shoulder as if God might be behind him waiting to judge. 'You know.'

'You're embarrassed about the charming André?' he checked, and she nodded. 'He's the cheat, Rachel, there's nothing there for you to be embarrassed about. So, are you going to let me in?'

'Oh.'

She was surprised he was at her door, let alone that he wanted to come in. She stepped aside and he looked very out of place in her shabby hall but very nice too.

'You wanted my phone number?' he asked her, to clarify.

'Yes.' Rachel nodded. 'Just to say sorry.'

'So you weren't hoping I'd ask you out again?'

'No.' She shook her head. 'I thought you'd left for overseas.'

'You're quite sure you didn't want me to take you out?'

'Quite sure,' she said. 'Anyway, you leave a week on Monday.'

'I thought you didn't like deep relationships.'

'I don't,' she agreed.

'And what if I told you I had tickets to see *Firebird* tonight?'

'Are you serious?'

'Always.'

Just not so serious when he was with her.

'How?'

Nikolai didn't answer.

After leaving Daniil's, he had intended to drive back to his yacht, get changed and go out.

He had felt lighter.

That his friends already knew had lifted his burden. He was looking forward now to Sev and Naomi getting back from their honeymoon, to catching up with old friends.

London was looking beautiful. The weather was warm, skirts were short and legs were long, and it was time to hit the town. He had some friends in London. Perhaps they could head back to the yacht and light up the night in his usual, wild style.

He hadn't partied since he had been here and that was unusual for him. He had been too busy thinking about Rachel.

And he had thought of her then, as he'd driven, and suddenly a wild night out had not appealed.

He wanted *her* to know the relief of another person knowing.

It was something he could not properly describe, but when he had told Yuri, the world had not only carried on turning, it had turned brighter.

And with Daniil's revelation, with the acceptance of a friend who knew, it had turned brighter again today.

Even if he was only here for a short while, he wanted Rachel to know that feeling so he had made a call and secured the hottest tickets in London tonight.

Rachel couldn't quite believe it.

'Did Anya give them to you?'

'No. I don't ask Anya for anything.'

'Why not?'

'I just never would. It is how we are with home kids.'

'Home kids?'

'The ones who have parents,' Nikolai said. 'So do you want to come to the ballet or not?'

'Want.' Rachel smiled.

'Then we have to leave now.'

'Now?' she said, and panicked when she realised the time and that she was still in her robe. 'I have to get dressed.'

'Then do so but...' As she turned to go he caught her wrist. 'I like these...' His other hand came to her face and his thumb went over her cheek.

'What?'

'The brown things.'

'They're called freckles, Nikolai,' Rachel said, but she blushed as she realised she had no make-up on. 'And they are not coming to the ballet.'

'Pity.'

'You call for a taxi, I'll get changed.'

She went into her bedroom and opened the wardrobe. She could shop for England and had plenty to choose from. She loved colour and standing out but tonight she was in the mood for something different so she selected a simple black dress.

She went into the drawer and chose demure underwear, some lacy cream knickers and a matching bra, and she shrugged off her robe.

'You need to hurry,' he called from the other side of the door as she put her underwear on.

'I am,' she said, and tried to keep the breathless note from her voice and to resist calling him in.

She was confused that he was here in her home,

dizzy that he had secured tickets to see *Firebird* and also terribly aware of her desire.

No, she didn't want a deep relationship but she ached for each moment with him.

She sat at her dressing table and reached for her magic foundation, and then she thought of his comment. She never went out without her make-up but tonight she went without foundation. She rouged her cheeks and then put on her eye make-up and mascara, and with little time she coiled her hair and pinned it up.

Her black dress she paired with nude shoes and then she stepped out. His eyes took in every detail, and her skin prickled under his scrutiny. She had dressed the most demurely she had since meeting him and yet somehow his eyes stripped her naked.

'Come on,' he said.

'Is the taxi here?' she asked, adding keys and lipstick to her bag and spraying her perfume.

'My driver is waiting.'

'Your driver?'

'Well, the firm I use when I am in London.'

She knew nothing about him, Rachel thought as she stepped into a luxurious car and asked a question. 'Where are you when you're not in London?'

'Here and there.'

'But where's your base?'

He didn't answer but Rachel took no offence—after all, there were loads of questions she chose not to answer—and so she spoke of the night ahead.

'I can't believe we're going to see Anya on her last night in London.'

She was so excited and it was infectious. 'Have you been to the ballet before?'

'Never,' he admitted.

'You are in for such a treat.'

'Will you write about it?'

'Oh, yes.' Rachel nodded. 'In fact, I make a point of writing about it the second I get home while it's fresh in my mind.'

It was then that he made up his mind. Tonight he would show her his—as Rachel called it—base.

Tonight he would invite her into his home.

The car pulled up at the theatre and the door was opened for them. And he watched as, after she climbed out, Rachel smoothed her hands down her thighs, as she always did. She was becoming familiar to him— delightfully so—and that was something he usually chose to avoid.

They were running late. The bell had been ringing for the audience to take their seats and they were swiftly shown through.

'How the hell did you get seats?' Rachel asked as they entered the packed theatre. She still could not believe it—even with all her connections in the dance world she had been unable to secure tickets for tonight. But then as the usher led them to their places and she took her seat beside a duchess, Rachel turned in confusion to look at the man beside her.

These were, Rachel knew, house seats—seats that the theatre kept aside just in case royalty, or a passing billionaire, suddenly decided at six p.m. that there was a production they wanted to see.

These were the seats that, when you performed, you knew might be filled by a princess.

'Nikolai...' she said. 'Where did you get the tickets?'

'Don't ask questions,' he said, as the lights went down. 'Just enjoy the night.'

Oh, she did.

Anya, or Tatania as she was tonight, was breathtaking.

Her slender frame was perfect for the part and when she performed a series of *fouettés* it was like watching a wisp of spinning gold.

Rachel had seen her perform on many occasions but tonight she was simply electric, like a feather on a breeze. Everything Anya had, Rachel knew, was poured into the performance tonight and they watched as she served up her heart for the audience.

Usually the interval was gratefully received but tonight the audience just wanted to be back in their seats. Rachel was torn. She wanted the performance to restart and yet, standing talking to Nikolai, hearing about Anya growing up, and just being here with him was unrivalled bliss.

'She used to practise in the kitchen,' he explained. Even he was impressed. 'Her mother was the cook at the orphanage and when Anya was home from a holiday she never let up, always she practised.'

'She's completely brilliant,' Rachel said.

'You're not jealous?'

'No.' Rachel shook her head. 'I just love watching her or any performer at the top of their game. I know I could never dance the way Anya does.'

'Because?'

'My height,' she said. 'It went against me in *pas de deux* classes. They don't want to risk the young males' backs…'

'You're tiny.'

'Not comparatively,' Rachel said. 'So, no, I always accepted I'd never be a soloist. Libby would be jealous of Anya,' Rachel mused, though she said it without malice, it was more an observation. 'She always wanted to play the lead.'

'What was your favourite part?'

'All of them,' Rachel said. 'I was never Odette but I was one of the swan princesses for a couple of seasons. The costume was so beautiful.' She sighed at the thought of it. 'It was just a swirl of white feathers and I felt like I was in heaven. Then I went back to being a swan. A happy swan! I just loved the chance to dance. Everybody has different ways of pushing themselves and trying to make it to the lead was one of Libby's...'

'What was your way of pushing yourself?' he asked, and Rachel thought about it for a moment before answering.

'Escape,' she admitted. 'I just loved the escape that dance gave me.'

'And without it?' he asked, as the bell rang to tell them to go back to their seats.

They ignored it for the moment.

Rachel was lost in her thoughts about what she would do without the escape the dance world had given her.

Since the age of five dance had ruled her and now she ruled herself.

What would she do without that escape?

'I have the right to remain silent,' she answered with a smile that was met by serious brown eyes.

'You do.'

Oh, the comfort that gave.

He didn't press her, he didn't demand to be led to her dark places; instead, he took her hand and they went back to their seats and again she was lost to another world, but not entirely.

She could feel him beside her, the warmth of his thigh and the heat of his hand that she gripped during a thrilling part of the performance.

And he held her hand tightly back, and she felt the pressure of his palm in her thumb and her stomach tightened.

'I don't want it to end,' she said as it did.

He let go of her hand and the crowd stood as one and cheered as the curtain rose and fell.

The applause was deafening and Tatania curtsied deeply and collected the flowers that were thrown, and then in a pause in applause Tatania suddenly stilled and looked up.

It was the only time in the entire night that she seemed frozen but she recovered and with one more curtsey she was gone.

'Do you want to go and see her?' Nikolai offered, and, given the seats they were in, Rachel *knew* it would pose no problem.

'No,' she admitted, because she had spent an afternoon, an evening and then a night next to him with others around and all she wanted was for them to be alone. 'I want to be with you.'

He was close behind her as they picked their way through the crowd and she could feel his eyes on her and then he took her hand again. How could holding hands be such a turn-on? Rachel thought as they walked. His touch made her want to run, with him.

They walked out on the street to where his driver waited when she would have preferred a kiss.

So would he.

Instead, they got into the car and sat apart because it was safer but still his hand was hot around hers.

'Where are we going?' she asked, as the car threaded through the traffic towards the Isle of Dogs rather than towards her home. She wondered if he had booked a hotel for tonight and there was a flutter of panic at the thought of staying awake for yet another night and the battle with the lights. At her flat she felt more in control, she could leave the hall light on... 'Nikolai, I have to go home. I need to write my piece...'

'I want to take you to my home.'

They climbed out of the car and there was a small crowd taking pictures of a luxury yacht that was lit up spectacularly.

'The Russians must be in town...' Rachel started a small joke and then halted as she realised that he wasn't taking her to some hotel, or some small apartment. The Russians were indeed in town and Nikolai's home was a superyacht.

They walked along a carpeted ramp and there were staff waiting to greet them.

It was like a luxurious hotel, but on the water, set over four levels. They took the stairs up and walked across the main deck and into the saloon.

She accepted a drink from a butler who then told Nikolai that dinner would be served soon and left them.

'How,' Rachel asked in her less-than-tactful way, 'did an orphan get this? I mean, house seats *and* a superyacht!'

Nikolai smiled as he shook his head. 'I'm not going to tell you.'

'Oh, but you are. I'm persistent, remember?' she said, but he would not be persuaded.

'Show me,' Rachel said. 'What's up there?'

He did show her. They went up to the sky lounge deck where there were guest rooms and a theatre and also a bar and dance area.

'I bet there have been a few parties held here.'

'A lot,' Nikolai agreed.

And she guessed a lot of women.

'Doesn't it worry you?'

'What?'

'That people might just want you for...?' Rachel shrugged. 'Well, for all this.'

'Why would it worry me?' He shrugged. 'It suits me. I don't want anyone around for long, so use away...'

'I just might!'

There was a gorgeous alfresco dining area with heaters so that, despite the cool night air, Rachel was warm even with bare arms.

'We could eat here if you prefer.'

It was odd, she thought. They headed up to the sundeck and she saw a Jacuzzi frothing. There was a massage room and a gym, all ready and waiting for them to use at whim.

Rooms waiting to be filled.

It was beautiful, it truly was, but it would be like being perpetually on tour—an odd sort of lonely?

'Do you have a captain?' she asked.

'I am the captain.'

'No, I mean a real one.'

'I am a real captain.' He smiled at her slight putdown. 'I have sailed far bigger ships than this. Here I have a first mate and there are two engineers...'

'And a cook?'

'A head chef and the sous chef...' Nikolai said.

It really was its own world, Rachel thought. 'Where's the control room?'

'I'll show you the helm station,' he said, and back down to the main deck they went.

He liked her questions and how she sat in one of the leather seats and looked at all the controls. He wanted her to see it all at its magnificent best—in the sunshine, out on the water—so he made her an offer.

'We could take her out for a few days, if you like. We would be back in time for the christening.'

'I can't get to the christening,' Rachel reminded him.

'Well, the wedding that you have to attend. How about it?'

'I don't think so.' She laughed at the very thought but then she fell quiet.

It was the nicest offer she had ever had.

Rachel was very well travelled, her career had seen to that, but the thought of a week spent drifting and indulging herself was appealing indeed.

And the thought of more time spent with him should have sealed the deal but it would mean sharing a bed. Oh, she might be able to stay away for the occasional night but not for a whole week. It was the reason she could not sustain a relationship.

It killed her to say no.

But she did.

'I've got a lot on this week,' she said. 'I promised to help Libby out.'

They both knew that Libby could find someone else but Nikolai chose not to push.

For now.

Instead, they walked through to the main saloon.

'What's up there?' Rachel asked as they passed some steps.

'I'll show you later,' Nikolai said.

'Ah, so it's the stairway to heaven, is it?' she said, and went to climb them.

'Later.'

She disobeyed captain's orders and went up and opened the door to, yes, heaven.

Oh, my!

The lights were like stars over the vast bed and the walls were glass. She had never seen a more beautiful bedroom.

He came up behind her and looked out at the view she was gazing upon. 'When you are out on the ocean and the water is smooth,' Nikolai said, 'you feel as if are lying on the water.'

She wanted to see it for herself and he knew it. He wrapped his arms around her and stood behind her.

She could feel his lean body and the strength in his arms and she wanted more of him.

He lowered his head and gave a small kiss to her ear and then spoke into it.

'Come away with me.'

But it wasn't only the dark she was scared of, it was the sudden thought of getting closer to him and then for him to be gone.

'I can't,' she said. He was kissing her cheek and she wanted to turn her head to meet his mouth. She leant back into him and felt him hard against her bottom, and then his hands moved down to her stomach and he pressed her in harder still.

His hands searched her body.

Kissing her cheek and her ear, deft fingers came to

her breasts and she loved his rough and thorough handling of them through the dress. She craned her neck so that their mouths could meet and he lifted the hem of her dress and slipped a hand into her knickers and played her.

Rachel almost couldn't kiss him, such was the bliss of his fingers. She leant deeper into him just to feel. She wanted to fold over, to lean against the window and be taken from behind, and she tugged down her knickers but Nikolai turned her around so that she faced him.

She went for his mouth, for a kiss, but instead she got his words.

'Why do you say no when we both know you want to come?' he asked.

'Oh, I want to come,' Rachel said, and stepped out of her knickers and kissed his taut lips.

'Rachel…'

He was persistent too, she thought, because how the hell could he attempt conversation while he was this hard?

'I don't want to talk.' She would end this conversation her way and she went for his zipper. Yes, Rachel always called the shots in bed, just not tonight.

He slapped her hand away.

'Get on the bed,' he said, and his voice was gravelly but low with command.

He started to kiss her hard and walk her backwards with his chest. And at the bed he sheathed himself and she would soon be pushed back. The air couldn't get into her lungs when she saw the dark desire in his eyes and she knew she was about to be thoroughly taken.

She was hot between the legs with want, absolute want for him, but her mind was awash with memories.

'Not the bed…'

He halted. He could see the flash of fear in her eyes and for a second he didn't understand it. Then he recalled the small tussle that had taken place in the last bed they had shared and he understood now that she didn't want to be underneath him.

Oh, she didn't. Rachel knew she had teased the tiger without telling the tiger her rules. A scream was building and she was about to ruin this perfect night with a shout of fear that he didn't deserve.

But then the scream died in her throat and changed to a shocked gasp as he lifted her.

Deftly he raised her and she jumped to his hands and secured her legs around him.

The relief poured from her mouth as she kissed him more deeply than she ever had. He entered her and she held his face and let him move her. His hands splayed across her buttocks and he moved her to *their* rhythm because they were one.

Nikolai loved her agility, the flex of her thighs that opened easily to him and then the welcoming tight grip of her.

One day he would do her long and slow, he told her in Russian, and she responded to his lust-laden words with her body and crossed her ankles behind him. She gave up on kissing, and as his hands moved to span her waist she arched back and his tempo increased.

He wanted her naked and Rachel too wanted to tear at her clothes just to expose her heated skin.

Even before Nikolai let out a shout, she felt the surge in his body, heard and then responded with a sob of her own. He gathered her into him as he released and she answered his intimate call with deep pulses that ached for him.

She would always ache for him, she knew as he kissed her.

And it took all that she had not to cry as he gently put her down.

He undressed her. Slowly, tenderly, and he put her to bed and then joined her.

'Dinner?'

Rachel laughed at the delicious suggestion and they were served lobster Mornay and champagne in bed.

'Where's my caviar?' she moaned, and peered under the shell as if looking for it. 'The service here is bloody terrible.'

And then she heard it, what she had never heard before.

The deep sound of Nikolai laughing. It was as beautiful as lightning yet it made her want to cry, because lightning was followed by rolling thunder, and she didn't want to count the time until the thunder arrived—the moment he would leave.

Their trays were removed and then it was just them and the night, and as Nikolai rolled over to flick a switch Rachel looked up at the ceiling and watched as the stars went out.

It was a different darkness from the one she was used to. The moonlight caught on the water and danced on the ceiling but it did not soothe her; instead, it shrank and then expanded the shadows and with the soft motion of the water beneath them it was disorientating.

His arm came over hers and he could feel her tension.

'Are you okay?'

'I am...' Rachel came up with an excuse. 'I haven't

written my piece about tonight. I should jot down some notes…'

'Why don't you just write the whole thing now?' Nikolai suggested. 'Use my computer.'

'You're sure?'

'Of course.'

He didn't need to turn on the lights and she heard him pad across the suite and then come back to bed with his laptop, which he handed to her. Rachel opened it up and sat in the glow of light and thought about *Firebird*.

There was so much to write, so many things to get down while she could still remember them. She tried to convey Tatania's amazing performance, how she was so light on her feet, just magically so, and how she had spun like liquid gold, how the Prince had seemed to love her even more dearly tonight, and how Tatania had given the performance her all.

Rachel read it back and her eyes started to get heavy. It was nice to work with Nikolai asleep beside her.

Relaxing even.

Too relaxing perhaps because a few moments later Rachel heard the soft thud of the laptop hitting the floor and realised she must have drifted off.

'Leave it…' Nikolai said, as she went to retrieve it.

It was kindly said, it was four in the morning after all, but without the glow of the computer she was back in the dark again with his arm over her.

If only she had left the laptop open, Rachel thought, at least then there would be some light.

Nikolai's hand moved and came to rest on her stomach and she looked at him in the darkness.

She was fighting sleep and how badly she wanted to simply give in to it and get out of the darkness and into her dreams, but she knew if his hand moved lower, if he touched her in her sleep she might scream.

Just stay awake, Rachel told herself, but awake on his yacht in the still of night was a scary place to be. The panoramic views from the master suite meant there was panoramic darkness and shadows and odd dancing lights that stretched and moved to the motion of the water beneath.

She felt sick.

How did you roll over and admit to a man you are terrified of the dark? Rachel wondered.

Maybe he sensed her panic, because he rolled in a little closer and she could feel him semi-hard on her thigh and soon he would want her again.

How do you tell a man when you've made love so passionately that in the dark just his touch could elicit a scream?

You didn't, she decided. You simply didn't.

Rachel wriggled of his embrace and quietly climbed out of the bed and tried to locate her clothes.

The yacht lurched a little, or perhaps it was her stomach, but Rachel found herself on her knees, feeling for her dress in the darkness.

Panic was starting to build and all she wanted was to be dressed and go home.

She found her dress and one shoe when she heard Nikolai's voice.

'What are you doing?' he asked.

'I thought I might go home...'

'Go home?' he checked.

'You did,' Rachel pointed out.

'We've already discussed that, you know why.'

His calm voice only accentuated her panic.

'I just want to go home.'

'It's the middle of the night.'

'I know that!' It was her least favourite time in the world.

'Rachel?' He started to say something but his words were drowned by the roar of panic in her ears.

'Nikolai.' She got up from her knees, clutching her dress, and told the truth she had never shared—she just blurted it out. 'I'm scared of the dark!'

CHAPTER NINE

THE STARS RETURNED.

The room was flooded with light and it felt like oxygen to her as she gulped in air.

She was always pale, Nikolai thought, but never more so than now. In fact, the panic in her eyes reminded him of years ago when he would wake up in the terror of recall. 'Come back to bed.'

'I can't.'

'I'll leave the lights on.'

'I don't want to fall asleep.'

'Do you get nightmares?

She was about to lie, to nod, but she had never lied to him so she told him a little of the truth.

'I don't like sharing a bed.' And she knew that made no sense. 'I don't like sleeping next to someone.'

'We don't have to sleep.'

He saw her eyes shutter as she assumed he was coming on to her but Nikolai wasn't suggesting that she get into bed for a sexual marathon. 'If you come back to bed, I'll tell you how an orphan like me got all this…'

He made her smile.

In the midst of panic he teased her with her own words and it drew her further away from fear.

'You said you would never tell me.'

'For you I'll break the rule.' And it always had been a rule for Nikolai. He never got in so deep with anyone to have that conversation. Times were changing, though, and soon he would be telling old friends his tale. He wanted Rachel to hear it first. 'Come on…' He offered his hand and she took it and got back into the bed.

There was icy sparkling water by the bed and he poured it into a glass and she had a drink and felt a little better still, especially at the soothing tone of his deep voice.

He asked for no more information and she was so grateful for that. Instead, he *gave* it. He told her about himself.

'I was fourteen when I ran away. I took the trans-Siberian train to Vladivostok. I was a hare…'

Rachel frowned.

'A stowaway,' he explained.

'But it's miles. How could you not be caught?'

'The passengers helped,' Nikolai said. 'They would hide me when the inspectors came, feed me. It happens on these trains. I got caught eventually and was kicked off. I waited two days for the next train and did the same again and I got to Vladivostok—the biggest port in Russia. It had always been my dream destination. I watched the ships for days and I chose the one I would go on.'

'As a stowaway?'

'Yes.'

It gave her goose bumps to think of it and she put down her glass and lay on her side, watching his lovely mouth and listening to his words.

'Well, I chose the vessel and I hid in the hold. I had

some supplies but when they ran out I would sneak out for food at night. I almost got caught when they offloaded in Japan but I had done my research and I hid in a pipe as they loaded more cargo. Once the captain had done his search the ship sailed again and I came out. It was all going well until the South China Sea, where there were pirates...'

Rachel's eyes widened.

'It happens. They wait till you slow down to navigate a channel and they approach on speedboats. They were armed.'

'What were they taking? The cargo?'

'No, these wanted cash and jewels. They wanted the safe open and all the payroll money. They robbed the crew and then shot them. When I came out, the captain, Yuri, was alive but not well.'

'Was he surprised to see you?'

'Nothing surprises a good captain,' Nikolai said. 'But he was cross. I found out later he had always prided himself on good inspections before sailing. Stowaways are a huge problem.'

'Like the lady whose baby you delivered.'

Nikolai nodded. 'That was years later but the problems are the same. If found they have to be repatriated at the vessel's expense.

'Anyway, though Yuri was cross, at least he could put me to work. Only a few crew survived and I was able to help. Under his instruction we got the vessel back to Vladivostok. I was terrified he would hand me in but, in the time it took to get back, we became friends, I guess. Once there he offered me some cargo—jeans, an awful lot of them. He would have it written off with the insurance. I could have been an oligarch.'

When Rachel shook her head to say she didn't understand, he explained a little better. 'I could have made my fortune on the black market, there was serious money to be had, but instead of that I asked him to teach me all he knew about shipping.'

'And he taught you?'

'Everything. For a couple of years I was a deckhand but then he had a contact and I headed north and worked on the icebreakers and had the best time. It was good money and it sorted out my head. These ships are so powerful they ride over the ice at speed, crushing it. It is magnificent but away from the ice, because of the hull, they are not so stable…'

'I want to go on an icebreaker.'

'You would…' He paused and then smiled at the thought of it. 'The power, the size, the speed… Sometimes you look behind at the path you've made and you are on the biggest, most powerful vessel and yet you are tiny. Even now, I love my time on them.'

'Is it lonely?'

'No, there are movies, meals together, it's a different life, and then there is time alone when you want it. Anyway, after my time on the icebreakers I headed back to Vladivostok and met again with Yuri.'

'How old were you then?'

'Twenty.'

She couldn't believe all he had done at such a young age.

'Then the real work started. I started to study for exams. Fourth mate, third mate, you have to have three hundred and sixty-five days at sea for each. Yuri taught me everything—I learned about maritime law, payrolls, customs, logging, forms and what a pain stowaways were. I made it to first mate and needed some more sea hours and on-board assessments to apply to be to a captain. I did all that and had just made it to captain when Yuri told me he was dying but he wanted one more voyage.'

'Did he have family?'

'He was a widower. He'd never had children. He said I was like a son to him and I considered him my family. I took his surname when I was eighteen.'

She had been right to be fascinated by him, Rachel thought. She could honestly listen to him for ever.

'That last voyage we drank a lot and spoke a lot and he taught me some more about life. He died where he wanted to and I buried him at sea.'

'Oh, no.'

'It was what he wanted,' Nikolai said. 'He was a good man. He missed his wife till the day he died and was ready to go. When he passed I found out that the icebreaker contact he'd had was, in fact, one of his employees. He owned two icebreakers as well as the merchant vessel that he died on. He was worth billions. All of it was passed to me.'

Rachel looked at him.

'He gave me everything.'

'He loved you like a son,' Rachel said. 'Are you glad you didn't take the jeans?'

Nikolai smiled at her response. 'I don't think you realise the money I could have made at that time with them.'

'But you wanted to work on ships?'

'From as far back as I can remember it was all I wanted to do. I always thought my father must have been a sailor. I was just born wanting to sail.'

'Now it's superyachts.'

'Mainly,' Nikolai agreed. 'But I still work the ice-breakers for a couple of months a year. The merchant vessel had to be scrapped. It was the hardest thing ever, she was a beautiful ship... That was when I moved into superyachts. I have three, the one I live on and the other two are for charter.'

'Do you still miss Yuri?'

'Very much. He's the only person I ever told what had happened to me at the orphanage.'

He watched as she blinked.

'I didn't want to but I was terrified of being sent back. I told him that I was being bullied but he knew there was more to it than that. He said, *"Beris druzhno ne budet gruzno"*—if you share the burden it won't feel so heavy.'

'Was he right?'

'Yes,' Nikolai said. 'I had so much anger in me and confusion. And he was so together and assured and the burden was so heavy.'

She almost told him, she almost felt she could tell him, but, as open as he was, for Rachel there was a deeper shame. That she must have enjoyed it—after all, she had sometimes come.

No, there were things you could never discuss.

He watched the struggle in her eyes and her mouth open and then close, and he remembered how hard it had been to tell another and he would not push.

Daylight was filtering in and he knew when to leave things.

'Go to sleep,' Nikolai said. 'I need to go and do some work.'

He left her then and she lay in his bed but didn't sleep for a long time.

Eight more sleeps.

And then he'd be gone.

CHAPTER TEN

THE BLISS OF her own bed wasn't quite so blissful now.

On Sunday night, after a delicious day, Rachel had been driven home at her request.

She was trying to play it cool as she tried to hold on to a heart that she had always kept locked away.

He would be the one to call her, she decided.

When, though?

And why would she want to get more involved when the simple fact was that he was leaving soon?

There was a knock at the door at ten on the Monday and Rachel was delighted to see a huge floral bouquet and did a little dance when she'd closed the door. With relish she opened the envelope and then sagged.

They were from the dance company, which was lovely, but she wanted them to be from him.

The afternoon and evening was taken up filling in as a dance teacher and just as she collapsed onto the sofa, the second she managed to go sixty seconds without thinking of him, her phone rang.

'How was it?'

His voice, his lack of introduction made her smile.

'The truth?' Rachel checked.

'Always.'

'I hated it,' she admitted. 'I am so not a natural teacher. Oh, my! First there was the baby class and it was so difficult to get them to focus, even for a minute. Then it was the mature age class. I think I overstretched them…'

He laughed and it felt like velvet in her ear.

And then he was silent.

'What did you do today?' Rachel asked.

'Some work, some thinking…'

'What are you doing now?'

'Why?' he asked, and she could not see his smile, but he knew she was waiting for him to suggest something.

'I'm just wondering.' Rachel shrugged.

'I'm watching the sun go down. I need your email address so I can send you the piece you wrote.'

She gave it to him and then attempted more small talk but Nikolai wasn't very good at that.

He had her email address. It was time to go.

Oh, invite me over, she thought, but refused to say it.

'Is that someone knocking on your door?' Nikolai asked.

'It is.'

'I'll let you go, then.'

He rang off.

It was him at the door, she decided. He was playing games and, delighted, she hauled herself off the couch, but instead of Nikolai there stood a man with a package to sign for.

She had no idea what it was, and even less of an idea as she opened the silver bag and there was no card, no note, just a tin…

A massive tin of caviar and a tiny mother-of-pearl spoon!

She broke every rule and rang him straight back.

'Don't speak with your mouth full,' Nikolai said, because she could barely get her thanks out, her mouth was so crammed with caviar.

'It's the best present!' she said. 'Better than flowers.'

'To make up for the breakfast I missed,' he said.

'Nikolai…' Yes, she was breaking every rule. 'When can I see you?'

'My driver's outside.'

She practically ran!

It was, without doubt, the most amazing week of her life. Better possibly than when she'd played the part of one of the swan princesses, because she was made love to by night and slept by day.

He turned her world upside down and she was dizzy with the excitement of it.

Even teaching difficult four-year-olds was fun with the knowledge that Nikolai's driver was waiting outside to take her back to his yacht.

She told herself that she didn't love him.

She insisted all week that it was just some necessary fun, as she did her best to convince herself she was still in control.

She was like a high-class whore and loving it, she thought as she locked up the dance studio on the Friday night and his driver held open the door.

Except this time Nikolai was in the back.

'I need to pop home.' Rachel smiled her toothy grin and she told him as they drove that she had an appointment with the dentist on Monday.

And a massage booked for Tuesday.

Distractions were booked in for the whole of next week, in fact.

Because he'd be gone.

'I shan't be long,' she said, and ducked out of the car, but he came with her.

And she was a terrible high-class whore because, and she didn't quite know how, they ended up chatting in her kitchen.

And when she should have been being wined and dined on his yacht and dancing in the moonlight, they were sitting on the floor of her lounge, eating a spaghetti she had made.

Of course, they ended up in bed, side on and naked, and she could not bear it that soon he would be gone.

She wanted to climb out of his embrace and slap his good-looking cheek, to think that he would leave her in this world without him.

But she didn't.

'I'll go,' Nikolai offered around one, because he knew she was tired and he did not want her pretending to sleep.

'Not yet,' she said, and then went to sit up. 'Your poor driver...'

'He's fine.' Nikolai laughed and pulled her back in.

'You can't just leave him out there.'

'What are you going to suggest, that he joins us?'

'No.'

Oh, she loved lying here in her bed in his arms with her head on his chest, stroking his stomach and feeling the warmth from him.

'Have you spoken to your mother about Sunday?'

Rachel shook her head. 'I tried but I can't. She's very...' Her nostrils tightened. 'It's better not to rock the boat.'

'What happens if you do rock the boat?'

'She falls apart,' Rachel said. 'Spectacularly so. Honestly, she's always been like it and I think her marriage is on the rocks, so we're due another drama any time soon.'

'How long has she been married?'

'To this one?' Rachel did a mental check. 'Three years.'

'Has she been married many times?'

'This is her third but there have been loads of boyfriends and...' Rachel rolled her eyes. 'I'd better not tell her about you and your billions. No one's off-limits in my family, no doubt she'd be coming on to you...'

'She wouldn't get very far.'

Rachel smiled and her eyes almost closed but she forced them open. The lights were blazing and she knew he liked the dark.

'I'm going to go,' he said, because if he didn't he'd fall asleep soon.

'Stay,' she said, because maybe she could be less scared of the dark with him beside her.

'Are you sure?' he checked. 'I don't want you faking sleep.'

'I'm too tired to fake it.'

She felt his soft laugh beneath her cheek but then she remembered that she feared a touch in her sleep even more than the dark and, yes, he had better leave.

Nikolai felt her tears fall on his chest.

'Go,' she said.

'I'm not leaving you crying. I'm going to stay.'

'I'm worried that if you touch me while I'm asleep, I'll freak.'

'Then I won't touch you.'

He made it seem simple and she remembered his

words about sharing the burden and maybe she could tell him. By her admission just now, she almost had.

And so she asked him something.

'Were you scared to run away?'

'I was more scared to stay, I guess. I just packed a bag and wrote a note and ran...'

'And they thought you'd died.'

'I ran down to the river. I wanted to get to the train station. I saw some youths fighting. One was pushed in and they all ran off. I was going to jump in, I dropped my bag and jacket but then someone stopped me. He said it was too late, and that if I went in there would two bodies. I knew he was right and I could hear sirens too. I didn't want the authorities to catch me so I ran again. I want to find out who he was.'

'You shall.'

Tell me, Nikolai thought, but when she said nothing, he revealed a little more in the hope she might open up.

'I took with me a ship I had spent years building...'

'Libby told me you built a ship from matchsticks.'

'Do you and Libby and talk about everything?'

'Not everything.'

'What don't you talk about?'

Rachel lay there and he tried again to get her to open up. 'You know the sexy book Daniil spoke about at the reception? I took that too.'

'Why?'

'To remind myself I liked women. These people mess with your head, Rachel.'

'Well, not for long,' she responded. 'You sorted yourself out.'

He had, she hadn't.

The difference between herself and Nikolai was that

he had done something about it. He'd had the guts to run away, and had left a note to protect others, when all she had done was lie there and pretend to be asleep.

No, she couldn't tell him.

Anyway, soon he'd be gone.

She felt his hand on her arm and he kissed the top of her head, and she lay in the light and listened to the sound of his breathing even out into sleep.

And she almost did the same but then a voice of the past popped into her head.

'You love it, don't you?'

Rachel could almost hear the voice of yesterday and feel her own shock and confusion that a man she loathed could bring her to orgasm. She went to sit up but Nikolai's arm was heavy over her so she lay there, catching her breath, feeling the soft stroke of his hand on her arm until, for the first time in her life, she slept with a man.

CHAPTER ELEVEN

TWO MORE NIGHTS.

Only it wasn't the happy countdown to Christmas or other such things, it was the appalling realisation, when she awoke, that in two more nights he'd be gone.

He had promised her just a week and that had seemed a good deal at the time.

Except she felt, as she lay there, as if she was adrift in the South China Sea and that pirates had invaded and captured her heart, her mind and a love she'd never thought she had to give.

He was stretching beside her and so sexy that she was happy he took up way more than half the bed.

'What's for breakfast?' he asked, and had she ever woken in bed with a man before and he had said that, she'd have given some smart retort, but instead she laughed.

'Caviar.'

She was on her second tin!

'Just tea for me.'

She had to climb over him to get out and she nearly didn't make it as they shared a lovely kiss with her sitting on his chest.

'Three sugars.'

'You're such a chauvinist,' Rachel said. 'Why don't you make the drink?'

'We're in your home,' Nikolai pointed out.

'Oh, and when we're on your yacht you have it served.'

'Feel free to use the galley when you're there if you prefer.'

And she would not be needy, she decided as she dunked his teabag, except she had to know and so as she walked back into the bedroom she asked him his plans.

'So where are you off to on Monday?'

'France,' he answered.

'You can go and see Anya perform,' Rachel said, doing her best to keep her voice light, but he shook his head.

'It doesn't open there for another month, I'll be long gone from France by then.'

She'd asked about his leaving and he'd told her.

And it hurt.

Nikolai sat up and took the cup and tried not to notice the disappointment in her eyes. He read her more easily than he had ever read anybody else.

They had agreed to one night and then they had agreed to a week. He had been upfront from the start.

So too had she.

But for Rachel things had changed.

'I'm going to have to kick you out soon.' Rachel did her best to keep her voice light. 'I'm getting my hair done at nine.'

'That's right, you have your leaving party today.'

'No,' Rachel said. 'I get my hair done every week. I hate washing it myself. There—another little thing about me you didn't know.'

There was a dig there, a small reference to last night, and he guessed she was embarrassed at having told him she feared a touch in the night.

He was wrong.

Rachel was *cross* with herself for trusting herself to a man who, in around forty-eight hours from now, was going to shatter her heart.

The phone rang and it was her mother. He drank his tea and listened to a one-sided conversation. 'Mum, Libby's baby is getting christened tomorrow and I—' There was a pause. 'I never said that I wasn't coming to the wedding but I was thinking, maybe if I just came to the reception...' And then there was a very long pause and he closed his eyes as Rachel gave in. 'It's fine, don't worry...'

It was painful to listen to such an assertive woman relent but it was not for him to say anything. Nikolai had no family and he certainly wasn't about to advise Rachel on hers.

She came back into the bedroom as he finished dressing.

'Oh, dashing off...' Rachel said, and there was a bitter ring to her tone.

They were descending into a row and he did not want that for either of them. 'You have your hair appointment. I have to sort things for my departure on Monday...'

Whoops, the M word.

But he did need to organise things. Nikolai wasn't an idle billionaire on a superyacht—he ran it, from the payroll to navigation...

As he went to leave, they were locked in pretence that things were normal and he moved in to kiss her.

But Rachel couldn't lie for a second longer, she couldn't give away even the smallest of kisses, not another shard of her heart, to a man who could not love her back.

She pulled back her head and denied him a kiss and her emerald eyes flashed in anger.

'Just go,' she hissed.

And he did so and it was at that moment, at the closing of the door, that she was sure she had lost him.

He woke up his driver with a knock on the window and was taken back to his yacht. There, as he charted the route they would take on Monday, he was conflicted. The first week here had been so long, the second, with Rachel, had sped by. He was used to short affairs, sailing off, literally, into the sunset without a backward glance.

Not this time.

Tomorrow Sev returned, and after the christening the three men would catch up.

He was looking forward to it now rather than dreading it.

And even if babies were not his thing he had enjoyed catching up with Daniil and Libby.

Even Anya.

There was history, there were shared pasts, and now he fetched the photo that Daniil had given to him and looked at it properly.

It was good to be back in touch.

More than that, it was good to be here.

He had always liked London when he had visited but never more than now.

For the first time there was a place that he didn't want to leave.

Or was it a person?

A woman who, like him, had been determined not to get too involved.

Except they were.

He had run away once, from the worst of things.

It felt now as if he was running away from the best.

He recalled her tense lips and the anger in her eyes that silently told him she was hurting, and in that moment, Nikolai knew, his love was born.

Rachel had her hair done.

It didn't help.

The hairdryer was too loud and the conversation grating.

She hated how they had ended and fought not to text him.

After her hair, she went to a luxury store to buy Nadia a little gift. She would go over next week with a cake and try to repair the damage to her friendship that not being at the christening would make.

Rachel knew exactly what she wanted to get and watched as a beautiful porcelain ballet figurine was nestled in its box. As she waited for it to be gift-wrapped she wandered around the store.

And there she saw it—a small crystal sculpture of a ship. It was so beautiful and intricate and absolutely perfect for Nikolai.

Why would she get him a gift?

Because she wanted to.

She let out a breath when she enquired the cost. It was way out of her league, just far, far too much.

And then she thought of how he made her feel in his arms.

And he'd lost his ship.

It wasn't about money, Rachel thought as she handed over her credit card and braced herself. This morning they had parted badly, tomorrow she had the wedding... Time was running out and she was wasting it by sniping.

She wanted to end things with a smile.

He deserved that much at least.

Happy with her purchase, determined to handle things better with Nikolai the next time they met, she headed to her own party.

Friends and colleagues were gathered and Libby had even brought along little Nadia. There was cake and champagne and all things forbidden.

Including André.

Rachel politely ignored him.

She cut her cake and that was followed by a couple of speeches and then the room went dark and she sat next to Libby and watched on the screen a montage of her career.

There was even footage of her at fifteen, when she'd received a full scholarship and had boarded. A little bit of school, a whole lot of dance. She could remember the relief at leaving home.

She'd been so young, Rachel thought as she watched herself, and anger seemed to clutch at her heart for what that bastard had done to that little girl.

'Give me a hold,' Rachel said to Libby, and she held Nadia and watched herself dance.

'Oh!' There she was as a swan princess and it was such a lovely memory. And there she was again, except on that night her costume had been too short.

'Remember they lost your costume.' Libby laughed.

'I might have to do a quick edit,' Rachel said, because she was so tall that that night her knees had been visible.

It was just a wonderful keepsake that captured all her dancing years.

And then it was over, and the lights came back on. It was the end of her career and Rachel truly didn't quite know where she was going.

In any part of her life.

'We really want you there tomorrow,' Libby said as she went to head off. 'I understand you have to go to the wedding but I just want you to know that you will be missed…'

'I know.' It actually broke her heart a little that she couldn't be Nadia's godmother; instead she would be at a wedding she didn't want to go to just because she didn't know how to say no.

'I'm going to have to get going,' Libby said.

'Thanks so much for coming.'

'Well, I was hardly going to miss your leaving party…' Libby said, and then stopped what she was saying.

Rachel was missing the christening after all.

There was a tiny wedge between them and Rachel understood why—they were close friends and the fact that she wouldn't be there tomorrow hurt.

People started to drift away and finally Rachel felt she could make her excuses and leave.

'I'll give you a lift,' André offered.

'There's no need.' Rachel tried to keep her voice light.

'Come on, Rachel.' André's voice was the voice of reason. 'We need to talk and surely it's better to clear the air now than at some Christmas dinner five years down the track.'

He was right, she knew.

It was better to say what she had to now rather than let it fester for years, and that was why she got in the car.

'We were never going anywhere,' André said as they drove towards her flat. 'You made it very clear that you didn't want to get too involved.'

'I know all of that,' she said, 'but now you're marrying my cousin. It's just not right.'

'Shona's pregnant,' André said. 'If she wasn't…'

'I don't want to hear that. I don't need to know that!'

Rachel stared ahead, it was hard to sort out the jumble of feelings in her head. André thought her jealous. She was so far from jealous and she did her best to articulate that.

'I'd just like to keep work and my private life and family separate and now every bloody Christmas, every wedding…' They had pulled up at her home and Rachel knew she wasn't doing a very good job of explaining things. 'I'm not just cross with you. Shona hasn't even given a thought to the fact that you're my ex. Does she know that we were still sleeping together when you met?' And then, because it really was a case of speak now or for ever hold your peace, she voiced a dark truth. 'I introduced you in Singapore. I didn't know you were seeing each other but I do know that we slept together after Singapore and I wouldn't have if I'd known you were seeing my cousin.' She was furious, embarrassed and appalled and she got out of the car and walked up her drive.

'Rachel!' André followed her. 'Don't storm off.' He came to the door. 'Look, you and I get each other. You don't want hearts and flowers, you've told me that, and just because Shona and I are getting married it doesn't change us.'

'What?'

'I get that you're hurting, but it doesn't have to change anything…'

Sometimes the things that hurt most didn't register at first. So stunned was Rachel as his mouth was on hers that she just stood there. His hand slid around her waist and he pulled her in just as thought surfaced.

He was getting married tomorrow and yet he would sleep with her today.

She just stood there, appalled.

Rachel could feel his mouth on hers and she wanted to recoil yet she stood there, only jumping when suddenly André jerked backwards.

It took a moment to register it was Nikolai who had pulled him off her and he had André literally by the scruff of his neck.

'Get inside,' he said to Rachel, and his voice was black with malice.

'I wasn't…' Oh, God, he'd seen her with André. Nikolai had seen André's tongue down her throat and… he was furious. 'We weren't…' she attempted.

'Get inside,' he barked his order.

She just fled into her house and a short while later Nikolai came through the door, a bit breathless and still very angry. Yet, instead of running from him, Rachel ran to him, desperate to plead her case, confused when he wrapped her in his arms.

And her reflexes were moving so slowly because

when he held her, when she was locked in his embrace, it took a moment to register that, yes, he was furious.

But not with her.

CHAPTER TWELVE

NIKOLAI WASN'T ANGRY with Rachel.

He had seen her expression when André had moved in on her and he'd recognised the fear and helplessness because he had known it too.

'I wasn't going to do anything, I wouldn't have slept with him…' Rachel pleaded, and then she knew he wouldn't believe her.

She didn't even believe herself.

Her head was spinning as it ran through scenarios.

He took her through to the lounge and she sat on the chair as Nikolai knelt down.

She remembered this morning and their difficult parting. The fact that he had come to see her should have her heart soaring, yet he had found her in another man's arms.

'I didn't know what to do,' she insisted.

'I know that.'

'You don't,' she insisted.

'Then tell me.'

'I can't,' she said, and she looked into brown eyes that waited patiently and wondered if she could. 'I just panicked.'

'And you could not move?' Nikolai asked. 'Like you

had no voice and that even if you spoke there was no one to hear it?'

He could remember the blast of the horn from the school bus and knowing it was pulling away and how he had just sat there immobilised by confusion and fear.

'It was like when my mother's boyfriend...' She looked down at her hands and his were wrapped around hers but she was quite sure that they wouldn't be soon. 'He kept coming into my bedroom. He would sit on the bed and say goodnight and at first he played with my hair. Sometimes I'd lie there and hear noises and I just told myself I was hearing things but then he started to touch me.'

She stared down at his fingers that stayed warm around hers as he asked her a question.

'Did you tell your mother?'

'I tried to,' Rachel said. 'I told her that he made me feel uncomfortable. But she got cross and said I was jealous that she was finally happy. She said I was always creating drama when there was none and that he treated me better than my own father ever did. She reminded me that he paid for my ballet, and do you know what?' She took a breath. 'A part of me didn't want him to leave her because I knew she'd fall apart again. She just can't live without a man in her life so maybe I didn't try hard enough to tell her. I don't know.'

'I do,' Nikolai said. 'She knew, she just didn't want to know.'

Yes, his hands were still there but they wouldn't be soon, Rachel knew, because she hadn't told him the worst part.

'I didn't want her to fall apart.' It was the black truth. 'And I wanted my ballet lessons.'

'Of course you did.'

'I wanted to get a scholarship and get out of the house for good. And that meant more lessons, private ones. I remember the term bill came and my mum was getting upset and he said it was too much and then the costume bill came in too. And then a quote for my braces. He said that I needed braces and said that he would pay for them...'

Rachel took a breath.

'I told him I wanted ballet, and I knew, as I said it, what would happen. That night I pretended to be asleep and he came in and said I didn't have to worry, he'd take care of the bill, and then instead of sitting on the bed he got in...'

'It's okay.'

'No, it's not. I'm not.' Rachel sobbed. 'I pretended to be asleep and it was awful but when he came in the next night I enjoyed it apparently...'

'Is that what he said?'

Rachel leapt with shame, she felt as if she wanted to climb out of her skin and walk off, to leave the carcass on the chair that could be painted pretty rather than reveal the wreck inside.

'Beris druzhno ne budet gruzno,' Nikolai said, and she wanted to believe him because the burden was so heavy.

'Sometimes I came.'

And she screwed her eyes closed yet she was sure even that could not shield her from his disgust. She almost expected a huff of revulsion, a slap to the cheek or the slam of the front door.

None of them happened.

She opened her eyes and Nikolai knelt there, the same as before, just the same.

He knew all about a body awoken too soon, and the guilt and confusion that made.

And he was still there and still the same. He held her as she spewed out all the conflicting thoughts and the terror and the shame of a body that had responded, and then she ranted at him.

'At least you did something about it. You ran away. I stayed, I just lay there and pretended to be asleep...'

'You did get away,' he said. 'You got your scholarship.' He just took the jumble of her mind and replaced it in a neater order. 'If it hadn't been the ballet he would have used something else. Did he remind you how bad your mother would be without him?'

She nodded.

'Mine told me that he would report Sev for cheating, that he would lose his chance to go to a good school.'

Rachel took a breath as Nikolai spoke on.

'I got away from that man just as you did. And the day I told Yuri was my hardest day but the best day because they keep you locked in a shame that is not yours to own. I thought my friends would think I liked it, or that I was gay when I knew I liked women. I didn't understand then that fear and forbidden and simple friction can make you come but that's not enjoyment. That bastard left you scared of the dark and a touch in the night, so clearly there was no real pleasure.'

Rachel opened her eyes to his and he was still there and, yes, she had shed her skin but it was not a carcass on the chair, it was her.

And he was there and had been through the same.

This strong, together man had once held the same fears as she.

She was suspended at fifteen.

Trapped in a guilty body, where every orgasm made her feel wrong and conflicted.

And she wanted to feel lighter, and she did.

Almost.

Not quite.

'Do you want to confront him?' Nikolai asked.

And that had been the dream. To return as an adult and face the man not as a child, to let rip, to unleash the anger she held inside her.

'Did you?' Rachel asked.

'I wanted to but then Yuri offered to take care of him. And I guess then I thought, no, I didn't want that. And I didn't want to see him again or give over any more of my life to him. I thought about it, though.'

So did she.

Every single day.

'Do you want me take care of him?' Nikolai offered.

Did he mean…?

Rachel was a little worried to verify just what Nikolai was suggesting but for the first time since her revelation her face broke into a smile and he looked at that lovely mouth and the gap in her teeth—she was so perfect to him.

'No,' Rachel said to his very kind offer. 'But thank you.' And she thought for a moment longer and maybe she would confront him but her mind was still dizzy.

'Will he be at the wedding?' Nikolai asked.

'No, no.' Rachel shook her head. 'They broke up a couple of weeks after I went to dance school.'

'I bet they did.'

She glimpsed his anger even if his eyes were kind.

She wanted to lie down and sleep but there was the burden of the wedding still to face. 'I don't want to go to the wedding.'

'Then don't,' Nikolai said, as if it really was that simple.

'I have to.' Rachel asked for help when she rarely did. 'Come with me,' she said. 'I'm not asking you to meet the family or a proper date or anything. It would just help if you were there.'

'I can't do that.' He shook his head. 'I'm not going to stand in a church and watch the groom wearing a black eye I gave him recite vows we know to be lies...'

'You blacked his eye?'

'I did,' Nikolai said, 'and I'll tell you something else. My knee has made sure he'll be black and blue in another place. It won't be a good wedding night.'

She almost smiled again but not quite. Rachel had asked just one thing of him and he had said no and he was adamant about that.

'It's time to start saying no to what you don't want and yes to the things that you do.'

'I can't say no. My mother...'

And that was it, Nikolai knew. Her voice had been ignored so much that she simply didn't know how to use it.

Except he was sure that she did: he believed in Rachel far more than she did.

He remembered the reason that he was here, the reason he had stopped by. He had spent the day not just thinking but acting on his thoughts.

Rachel didn't need to hear them now.

He could see that she was near to tears and holding them in, just as he had when he had finally told Yuri.

She needed time, and to sort her head out, and yet she needed to sort it out fast if she was going to get out of going to the wedding.

He could stay, push for her to see sense, but Nikolai did not operate like that. He wanted only the best for her and that was to work things out for herself.

And he knew how.

He removed his hands from her and held her cheeks between his palms.

'You have to do what's right for you.'

'I know.

'Nikolai…' She wanted to ask him to go with her tomorrow again but she was too proud to ask twice. But then, just as she went to be brave, to ask him to reconsider, his lips came to her mouth.

He was kneeling and moved in closer and it was a deep sensual kiss with his tongue slipping into her mouth. It was a slightly possessive kiss. Perhaps, Rachel thought, he was making his claim after André.

And there was longing, there was always longing when there was Nikolai, but as his body moved closer as she went to kiss him back, to part her knees so he could move in closer still, the oddest thing happened.

He felt the roll of her tongue, and then it stilled.

'Nikolai…' She pulled back. She had just told him the darkest, most difficult part of her life, she had just been pounced on by André and, well, it was insensitive at best to move in for a kiss. And, given his hands were now moving down from her face and up her dress, it was more than a kiss he had in mind.

'Not now…' She just said it.

'Sorry?' he checked.

'I just...' Rachel felt his hands halt their roaming of her thighs. 'I think I need some time.'

'Time?' Nikolai frowned as if he didn't understand what she meant.

'I'm not really in the mood for doing it on the chair!' Rachel snapped, and made things very clear. She was cross. Oh, yes, he'd been lovely and everything while she'd told him but really! 'I just told you...' Oh, she didn't want to go over the abuse stuff again, so she moved on to another slight. 'I just asked you to come to the wedding. It took a lot to ask you...' Oh, what was the point? Rachel thought. 'I need some time to think.'

'And you can't do that with me?'

'Not with your hands up my dress,' she snapped. 'Can you just go?'

'You want me to leave?' Nikolai checked.

'I do.' She stood and smoothed down her dress over her thighs in the way he adored.

'You're sure,' he checked. 'Or we could—'

'I'm sure, Nikolai.'

She even held the door open for him.

'Text if you need anything,' he offered.

'Sure.'

'I mean it.'

And only when he'd gone and Rachel stood in the hallway alone did she finally break down and cry.

He stood on the other side of the door for a few moments and heard the dam break and the wretched sound of her tears. He fought the urge to go back in there.

He had curled up on the bed after he had told Yuri and that had been the last time he had cried, as he had let go of the past. And then, the next morning, there had been a knock on the door and Yuri had put his head around and had told him he was late and to get to the galley and make breakfast.

A new normal.

He had walked out of that cabin a different young man.

Yes, Rachel needed that time by herself, so he headed to his car and back to his yacht.

Years later Yuri had told him he had sat all night wondering if he'd said the right thing, wanting to check that Nikolai was okay while knowing he'd needed space.

Yes, he had been by himself but someone who'd cared had been thinking about him.

So Nikolai sat and drank vodka infused with ginger with his phone by his side.

Rachel was by herself, but she was not alone.

His mind was with her all through the night.

Oh, she needed to cry, not for him but for the fifteen-year-old she had been and for nearly two decades of guilt and shame that she had lugged around with her.

Rachel cried and cried and then she got angry.

And then she started going through the computer, trying to find his name and where he lived, and she had visions of driving across London and…

Except, like Nikolai, Rachel didn't want to hand over yet another chapter of her life to him.

She didn't want to be sitting in a police station a few hours from now, explaining why she'd run the bastard over or kicked in his door.

She wanted her life to start.

A new life, free from the past.

Yes, she wanted to fall into her life and suddenly felt calmer.

Calmer than she could ever remember feeling.

And it turned out that Yuri was right, because Rachel felt lighter.

She thought about texting Nikolai, to thank him for listening, but then remembered that she was cross with him for the hand-up-the-dress moment.

Bloody men, Rachel thought, very glad she'd said no.

She'd said no!

And she could do it again.

So instead of tracking down the address of her abuser, she picked up the phone.

'Hi, Mum.'

'Oh, you'll never believe it,' Evie said. 'Mary just rang and poor André got jumped on his stag night...'

Rachel rolled her eyes at André's quick attempt to cover the mess Nikolai must have made of his face. 'Mum,' Rachel took a breath. 'I'm not going to be at the wedding.'

'Don't start.'

'Mum, I used to go out with André—'

'Oh, here you go, creating drama. That was ages ago.'

'We were sleeping together right up till you told me he was engaged to Shona.' She chose not to tell her mother about afterwards, or what had gone on tonight— not that it would have made a difference, Rachel thought as her mother carried on.

'Rachel...my sister has been good to me and if you think for a moment I'll let you ruin her daughter's—'

'Mum,' Rachel broke in. 'I've been asked to be Nadia's godmother and I want to be. I take it very seriously. I want to be there for her if she needs me and that starts now. I want her to be able to talk to me—'

'Rachel—'

'No,' Rachel interrupted. 'I am not going to the wedding. I am not turning my head away and pretending nothing is wrong, or nothing awful is happening. You can,' Rachel said. 'But I won't. Ever. I'm going to be the best bloody godmother I can possibly be...'

Unlike you.

She didn't say it, but there was a silent dare in Rachel's voice for her mother to push this conversation on.

She had a voice and she would use it now.

'Well, it sounds as if you've made up your mind,' Evie said.

She had.

And she had made her mind up about other things too.

First she texted Libby and said that she would love to be there tomorrow and, if it didn't cause too much trouble, she would be thrilled to be Nadia's godmother.

Then she took the article she had written about the closing night of *Firebird* and put it up on her blog and hit 'Publish'.

It was done.

She put out her outfit for tomorrow and the gift that she had bought for Nadia, and she knew that she'd lied, not just to Nikolai when he'd asked but to herself. She *did* want a baby of her own. She had been terrified she might not be a good mother. But she would be, she knew it now.

They could both have night-lights, Rachel thought with a smile, then it wavered as a fresh batch of tears came.

Not shameful tears, not even angry ones.

Just sad ones about the man she would miss for ever.

CHAPTER THIRTEEN

A NEW NORMAL.

Rachel lay in the bath, with rollers in her hair and teabags on her eyes, and the anxiety that had been her cumbersome friend for so long was gone.

She was both looking forward to today and also dreading it.

Godmother to little Nadia, being amongst friends, instead of some nightmare family function, it was a perfect day.

Apart from Nikolai leaving.

Still, she was not going to let that ruin things for her or her friend so she hauled herself out of the bath.

She took out her heated rollers and while her hair cooled she dressed carefully for the christening. Last night she had chosen her lovely willow-green dress teamed with subtle nude shoes. This morning she changed her shoes to very high-heeled sandals that were a bit tarty for church, but they were too good to stay home!

She put on her make-up and examined her teeth and remembered that tomorrow she was going to the dentist to see about braces.

Yet that gap seemed less important now.

A taxi took her to the church and there was a flurry of nerves in her stomach as it pulled up and she looked out of the window.

'Just give me a moment,' Rachel said.

It was going to be so hard to say goodbye and she wanted just a moment to nail on her smile.

There were Sev and Naomi back from their honeymoon and Libby and Daniil speaking with Anya.

And there was Nikolai.

So beautiful.

He was dressed in a dark suit and was clean-shaven, and he was talking to Libby, seemingly without a care in the world. He looked more relaxed and happy than she had ever seen him.

It just didn't seem fair that he could be so together when her heart was breaking, but she was, Rachel vowed, going to do this right.

The last two times she had said goodbye had been awful.

She thought of the tense dodging of his kiss yesterday morning and then holding the door to let him out last night.

It had been sex to him and she got that.

He had been everything to her and she would say goodbye nicely the third time. She would give him the gift and thank him for all he done for her.

Because, yes, even with a broken heart she felt lighter.

She got out of the taxi and walked towards the gathering, her smile firmly in place.

Libby, holding Nadia, broke from the group and almost fell on Rachel's neck she was so pleased to see her. 'Oh, I'm so glad you made it. Do you have to dash off after?'

'No, no.' Rachel shook her head and then looked down at the baby.

She was wrapped in the blanket that Rachel had bought her and was asleep and content and just beautiful.

'Can you imagine Anya as godmother?'

They shared a little laugh.

'We've got an extra guest,' Libby told her. 'You'll never guess—' But Libby didn't get to finish because Anya, Queen of Ice, had made her way over and actually kissed Rachel on both cheeks.

'I read your piece,' she said. 'It was amazing. Rachel, I will be in touch and we'll have to see what we can do about tickets for opening night...'

Oh, my!

Then Anya turned—in fact, they all did as a car drew up and, no, Rachel really couldn't keep up.

Was that Daniil getting out of the car?

But, no, he was already here.

It was Roman!

'Oh...' Rachel said. 'Isn't he the missing one?'

'He was never missing,' Anya scoffed. 'He's been in Paris.'

'You knew where he was,' Libby accused. 'And you didn't tell Daniil...'

'You've heard of Russian mail-order brides,' Anya sneered. 'Roman was a mail-order groom to some bored, rich, middle-aged woman in Paris...'

'No.' Rachel started to laugh.

'Oh, yes,' Anya sneered. *'Alfonso...'*

She turned as she felt Nikolai beside her. 'What does *alfonso* mean?' Rachel asked.

'Male gigolo.' He smiled too but then he was serious. 'You made it.'

'I did.' Rachel nodded. 'I rang my mum and told her...' She gave a little shake of her head. 'It doesn't matter. You look very nice!'

He did.

Nikolai was dressed for a wedding, in fact.

Yes, despite harsh words yesterday he had decided he would watch the baby get dunked, race across the city to be at the wedding and by Rachel's side then race back to catch up with Sev.

Which was supposed to be the reason he was here after all.

But those reasons had changed now.

He looked down at a woman who had made it. He had read her piece online about two this morning and was very, very proud of her.

Yes, his mind had been on her all night.

'I see you published your work. Anya's been glowing...'

'I did.' Rachel nodded and then she did another brave thing. 'Could we talk after the christening party? I know you're heading off tomorrow, I just—'

'I'm going to be meeting with Sev and the others,' Nikolai said. 'He flies back to New York later tonight and they're going to come back to the yacht so we can catch up.'

'It's fine.' Rachel shook her head. She had wanted to say thank you, to give him his gift, but she couldn't do that here without crying.

'Maybe come over after they've gone,' Nikolai suggested.

Oh, yes, she thought, remembering how he had tried it on last night.

'I don't think so.'

'Up to you.' Nikolai shrugged and walked off.

She'd get a bloody refund on his ship, Rachel thought, and let out an angry breath.

And then she let it go. After all, there was a special star today.

Nadia Rachel Zverev.

That made her cry.

It was a lovely service and Rachel was so glad that she had made the effort to be there. Instead of dashing off after the service to be at a wedding she did not want to attend, she found herself back at Libby and Daniil's huge apartment.

There was chatter and laughter and pink cupcakes and champagne.

Pink everything really!

As the gathering started to thin out Nikolai looked out at the view. It was the same as last week, only different also—two warm weeks meant that clouds were gathering. A storm to clear the air was brewing and from this penthouse apartment it would be a spectacular sight.

Nikolai loved to watch storms from the theatre that was the ocean, to be in it, to feel the roll of the waves and the power of nature unleashed.

Rachel came and stood by him and he turned and gave her a smile.

She was a storm in his life.

And Nikolai loved a good storm.

He saw she was holding little Nadia.

'For someone who doesn't want babies,' Nikolai commented, 'you can't put her down.'

'She cries when she's put down,' Rachel told him.

And, yes, so would she.

But not in the same way as before.

They would be healing tears she would weep, not regretful ones. She didn't regret a thing about her time with Nikolai. Even what had happened with André had pushed her to a better place.

'I think I've changed my mind about not wanting babies.' She saw his slight startle. 'Don't worry, Nikolai, we've been careful and I'm on the Pill. I shan't be calling you on your satellite phone or Morse coding you...' She saw his tiny frown. 'Or semaphoring you that I'm pregnant...'

She *did* make him smile.

'You could always just send a text.' His response was dry.

'I like the semaphore idea,' Rachel said.

'Am I taking away your drama again?'

They smiled and were back to their first lovely night. He so calm and unruffled, she so dizzy and making shapes in the darkness of her mind.

'Thank you.' Rachel said what she had wanted to in private. 'Thank you for an amazing couple of weeks and for...' No, she was not going to cry here.

'As I said, you can thank me in person tonight.'

'I don't think so.'

She wanted more than one-night stands and casual relationships now. She went to go into her bag to, hopefully, slip him his gift discreetly, but she was interrupted.

'Nikolai...'

They turned at the sound of his name and, now that the party had thinned out, it was time for the men, after all these years, to catch up.

That was the reason he had stayed these two weeks, Rachel reminded herself.

She had been but a little stopgap and yet she could not resent that.

'If you can't make tonight, what about tomorrow?' Nikolai said.

'I've got the dentist tomorrow,' Rachel sighed. 'Mind you, if I'm thinking babies maybe I shouldn't be blowing all that money on my teeth…' And then she blinked and smiled. 'That's my first ever unselfish thought.'

'I think you are far from selfish.'

'Oh, I am,' Rachel said. 'I say and do the right thing but I seethe with resentment.'

They shared a smile.

'Breakfast tomorrow?' Nikolai offered.

'I don't know,' she admitted, and it had nothing to do with cancelling the dentist, it was going to be hell saying goodbye. Maybe it would be better here, just get it over and done with, but she wanted to give him his ship and she wanted to be alone with him, just one more time. 'Breakfast.' Rachel nodded. 'Shall I come to you?'

'No, there is somewhere I want to try…'

He gave her the name of a swanky place in Belgravia and, yes, it was lovely but a bit public, so clearly they'd be keeping their hands to themselves.

Which was what she wanted, wasn't it?

'That would be lovely,' she said, and smiled as she, of course, seethed!

'Tomorrow,' Nikolai said, and walked off, and Nadia

let out a loud wail, which was just what Rachel wanted to do.

'I'm going to feed her and then put her down for a sleep,' Libby said, and Rachel started to hand Nadia over to her but instead she carried her through.

Libby took Nadia out of her gown and changed her into a little sleep suit and, after such an exhausting day, and a very quick feed, she was soon asleep.

'I want one,' Rachel whispered, as she gazed at the baby.

'I thought you said never...'

'I know I did.' Rachel nodded. 'It's your duty now to talk me out of it. How was it?'

'How was what?'

'We haven't caught up since the wedding. Well, not properly. You haven't told me a thing about the birth!'

They crept out of the nursery and it had turned dark, but instead of turning on the lights they sat and ate cupcakes and drank champagne to the spectacular backdrop of the storm, with Rachel laughing and squirming as Libby told her in painful detail about Nadia being born.

And then the conversation turned to Rachel.

'So Anya came up with a ticket for you for closing night?'

Rachel nodded rather than correct Libby. Oh, tomorrow when he was gone, new baby or not, she would be round here with her friend passing the tissues, but right now she wasn't ready to share.

Or maybe tomorrow, instead of crying on Libby, she would head down to the wharf and look at the space where his yacht had been, Rachel thought, and then dragged her mind back to the conversation. 'She's going to see about tickets for opening night in Paris!' Rachel said.

'Ooh, you might see Nikolai. He told Anya today that he'd see her in Paris. Do you think there's something going on there?'

Rachel just shrugged. She knew there was nothing going on between Nikolai and Anya, it was just that Libby, in new-baby land, was completely out of the loop.

'I guess they just want to keep in touch.'

So did she.

Already her mind was leaping ahead to Anya's opening performance and the chance of a night spent in his arms.

She had that chance now.

It had taken just two weeks to change her life and he had been such a part of it that she wanted to say goodbye properly.

Maybe she could head down there now but she knew where that would lead and she'd given up casual sex.

She was reaching for her bag.

Her casual sex ban had lasted less than twenty-four hours.

How pathetic was that?

But it wasn't.

She wanted one more night with him.

CHAPTER FOURTEEN

LONDON LOOKED SHINY and clean after the storm and as Rachel got out of the taxi she saw his yacht and her heart felt as if it was in her mouth.

It was all lit up and it matched the beauty of the sunset.

Golden lights glinted on the water and Rachel remembered lying in bed and watching the reflections dance along the ceiling.

She'd been scared then.

Not now.

There was a little crowd gathered and Rachel joined them and did as they did—took a picture of *Svoboda*.

Freedom.

Nikolai had given her that—freedom to be herself and to let go of the past.

She didn't blame him for moving on. That had been the plan from the start and given what had taken place yesterday between herself and André...

Rachel closed her eyes for a brief moment. She wished Nikolai hadn't had to have seen that.

She sat down on a bench and heard someone complaining that the car hadn't been taken out.

'Is that what you're waiting for?'

'Yep,' the man said. 'The car was designed as an accessory to the yacht...'

Rachel's eyes glazed over as he droned on and on about hydraulics and then blinked as he snapped her back to attention. 'So what are you here to see?'

'The captain,' Rachel said, and went into her bag and offered her new friend a chocolate éclair sweet.

It was a very long wait. The four men had a lot of catching up to do, Rachel guessed. In fact, she was down to her last sweet and had passed the time learning maritime-speak on her phone when finally there was a bit of movement in the crowd. Rachel looked up and there was a sigh of disappointment when the car didn't come out; instead, three, a little worse for wear, sexy Russians disembarked and one, none the worse for wear, remained.

He did not stay behind the tinted glass walls; instead, he came out to the bridge deck and watched his friends leave.

They had caught up, filled in the missing years, and it was then that Nikolai saw her—sitting on a bench and chatting to a man by her side.

For Nikolai she had the spotlight, always.

He sent her a text and watched as she went into her bag and then laughed as she read it.

Get here!

She stood up and he watched as she hitched her skirt down her thighs and then walked over, and he went down to greet her.

'I know it looks a bit stalkerish...' she said as she

stepped on board. 'I just didn't want to interrupt you all. Was it nice to be together again?'

'It was,' Nikolai agreed. 'Though I'm glad you came.'

'We deserve a nice goodbye,' she said, and he realised that she was here to say farewell to him with a smile.

That was brave.

'So tell me,' Rachel asked, 'how were they?'

'I don't want to talk about them.' He wanted to talk about *them*, but Rachel's eyes had lit on a rather odd-looking object for such sumptuous surroundings.

There was an ugly little varnished ship on a coffee table.

'Is that the ship you built?' Rachel asked.

'It is.' Nikolai nodded. 'Sev kept it all these years and had it couriered to London while he was away. He just gave it to me.'

She walked over and picked it up and looked at the hundreds of matches. She thought of him as a child with a dream, but instead of telling him it was amazing she pulled a face.

'Bloody Sev,' she grumbled.

'Why is that?' he asked the woman who never said the words he expected yet always made him smile.

'Well, it was very thoughtful of him but it kind of messes up my present.' She went into her bag and handed him a box, which he opened and stared at the little crystal ship that lay inside it on dark velvet.

He looked at the beauty and fought with instinct to say that it was too much, or that she shouldn't have.

She should have and she had.

What they had found had nothing to do with money.

He put the little crystal ship beside his matchstick one and tried to find the words to thank her.

All those years ago he might have dreamt of a better future but he could never have imagined this.

'It's beautiful,' Nikolai said, and he looked up at her. 'It's the nicest gift I have ever had.'

'Really?'

'Absolutely.'

And impulse purchases had their rewards because she got the heaven of hearing this: 'If everything went down, this would be the one thing I'd save...'

'You're the captain,' Rachel said. 'Aren't you supposed to go down with the ship?'

'I have to see everyone off first, then I can get off.'

'Well, you'd be told off for stopping to retrieve your possessions.'

She made light of it, though her heart swelled at his words, and in that moment Nikolai knew just how precious the gift was that he had just received.

She really was here to say goodbye—it was a gift with no strings, it came from the heart. He wanted to correct her, to say that this could not be goodbye, but for now he listened as Rachel spoke on. 'I'm just sorry for what happened yesterday...'

'Why are you sorry? I'm glad that you told me what happened to you.'

'No.' Rachel shook her head. That wasn't what she had meant. She was glad she had told him too. It was what had happened before that. 'I'm sorry you had to see André and me. I just...' She let out a breath. 'I'm very glad you came when you did...'

'Rachel,' he said, 'you wouldn't have slept with him.'

'I don't think so. In fact, I'm very sure of it, but I understand that you might doubt that.'

'No.'

He had more faith in her than she had in herself.

'I know for a fact you wouldn't have,' he said. 'You were just shocked...'

'I know I was,' she agreed. 'I didn't know what was happening.'

'He did,' Nikolai said. 'But, Rachel, you're past all that now. It might have taken you a couple of moments to re-group but you would have slapped his face and seen him off.'

'I would have.'

'You would have,' he confirmed. 'After all, you had said no to me.'

Indeed she had!

'And you fancy me a lot more than him.'

'You know that, do you?' she teased.

'I do.' Nikolai nodded. 'Yet you still said no...'

'Well, I just thought it was a bit insensitive given all I'd told you and...' She halted and then her eyes narrowed as she started to see yesterday in a different light. 'You set me up to say no.'

'I did!'

'So all that time I thought you were an insensitive bastard you were...' She put her arms around his neck as he spoke for her.

'You know how to say no.'

'I do,' she said. 'Can a lady change her mind?'

'It's her prerogative.'

There was so much he had to tell her yet there was no chance of that now because Rachel was claiming her kiss.

One more night with this man and she would not waste it.

Tomorrow it would kill her.

The morning would see her back on the bench, watching the little tugboats sail him away, but tonight she would let herself love him.

It was a different kiss from any they had shared for she did not kiss from the groin.

Instead, she tasted his lips as if they were the rarest and most precious of wines, or vodka infused with ginger, or just Nikolai and a man who kissed her in a way no one ever had.

He held her cheeks and kissed her back, no tongue, just soft, velvet kisses, so soft that she had to close her eyes to keep the tears in. His hands moved into her hair and he kissed her harder now, and she parted her lips as his tongue came in, yet it was still a tender caress.

They undressed each other slowly. Rachel refused to rush because she wanted it to never end. And so, when they stood naked and pressed into each other, when deeper, sexier, more wanton kisses came, when she did not want it over, when she lay on the bed, instead of trying to bring them both to conclusion, she let him linger.

It hurt to be kissed so gently, to be made love to by a tender mouth. Gentleness was something she had never allowed herself to experience, but as his mouth worked her breast, as his fingers intimately stroked her, he banished dark memories and replaced them with bliss. Her breasts he explored with his mouth and Rachel's hands were on his head, pressing him into her flesh as her hips lifted to his hand.

His mouth moved lower and so did he, so that he

knelt on the floor, and she looked up at the ceiling with her mouth open wide, stunned not just at the utter delight he gave but the access to herself she permitted.

Sex had never been guilt-free and as she came to his mouth it wasn't quite guilt-free now. There was the rush of pleasure and the sink of oblivion and then she closed her eyes.

And she waited.

For the voice that told her she was wrong, that the pleasure she sought was forbidden, but Nikolai came over her and it was his voice she heard in her ear.

'You mean the world to me.'

And his world was a complex one, Rachel thought as she looked into his eyes. His world was a vast one that he travelled, but he was here tonight. He kissed her and she tasted herself and then him. His weight on top of her did not make her want to roll away, it felt right.

He was on his elbows and looking down at her, and what a difference that made. To look into his eyes as he took her and not to deny what was taking place but to want it.

She remembered him slapping her hand away as she'd gone to stroke him but then he'd banished the memory and let her hold him. And she let him love her now.

'Oh!'

That was what she said as he slid inside and filled her.

And her eyes stayed open and looked right into his. She tried to reach for his mouth to kiss him but failed. Her body just caved in to the delicious sensations and then rose to match his.

Nikolai took her slowly but deeply, every thrust measured, and she started to moan from the pleasure. Her hands came up to his shoulders and she felt the hard muscles and the tension he held as he tried to keep things slow, yet Rachel was ready now to be taken thoroughly. Her legs wrapped around him and her arms pulled him down, accepting the collapse of his weight onto her.

And when he consumed her, when it was now just the two of them in their minds, he thrust harder and faster and she begged for the same.

'Nikolai.' She said his name as she started to come but she held on to the three words no playboy wanted to hear.

That she loved him.

She came so hard that it felt as if she was attached to an electricity grid as her body went rigid. The most intense pleasure was magnified as he moaned his release and shot into her and she came again. She just tipped straight back into orgasm and forgot how to breathe. And then, as it faded, as he emptied the last, she opened her eyes to him and smiled.

No guilt, no shame, nothing other than a smile for the beauty they made.

'Double,' Rachel said, as if he didn't know.

'Extra shot.' He smiled back and they laughed at a joke in their private language and he kissed her.

How would she stand it when he'd gone?

It was hard to lie next to the love of your life and not tell him that he was, in fact, that.

They lay there, all lights blazing, and Rachel was deep in thought. Her limbs felt heavy, her mind, though, was whirring and wondering how the hell she would get over him.

She wouldn't.

She knew it.

Oh, she'd smile and pretend that she had but there would never be another him.

'What?' Nikolai asked, as if he knew she had something to tell him.

'Nothing,' she said.

Everything.

She blew out a breath and wondered if she dared tell him a little of what she was feeling.

But how?

Maybe it would be easier in the dark but she hated it so.

Nikolai turned and went to the bedside table, but instead of plunging them into the darkness he rolled back and held out a slim pouch.

'What's this?'

'I got you a present too.'

'What is it?' Rachel asked as she sat up and pulled out a slim piece of black velvet. 'An eye mask.' She gave a slightly mocking laugh. 'I think I'm the worst person to give an eye mask to. I can think of nothing worse than being blindfolded...' She shot him an incredulous look. 'That is the most thoughtless gift ever. I hate the dark, I—'

'It's for me,' he said, and took it from her hands and put it on. 'You can keep the lights on.'

'Oh.' She looked down where he lay beside her, clearly settling into sleep.

'Not so thoughtless, after all,' he said with a smirk.

'I guess.'

She lay back down beside him and he held her in his arms and she looked up at him. As lovely and thoughtful as his gift was, she wanted to see his eyes. Even closed they were such a beautiful part of him so she did the bravest thing. She turned off the lights and lay there, watching the flickering shadows on the ceiling, not scared of the dark with him by her side.

She took the mask from his eyes and then lay in the darkness.

'I won't touch you while you sleep,' he promised.

'Thank you.'

He just held her instead and then, as she was drifting off, he remembered all that he hadn't told her, and all the plans he had made. He glanced at the clock and saw that it was almost midnight.

Oh, well!

He sat up and then came her sleepy voice. 'It's fine,' she said. Assuming that the sudden startle from him was because he had just realised that they hadn't used a condom. 'I'm on the Pill.'

He didn't respond and Rachel sat up blinking as the lights plunged on and he made a call and then spoke on the intercom to his butler.

'Why is he preparing the car?'

'Because there is something I want to show you.' Nikolai said. 'Get dressed.'

'It's nearly midnight,' she pointed out, but got out of bed and did as he asked. After all, she didn't want to sleep their last night away. 'Do you know they're all waiting on the dock for you to take the car out for a spin?'

'I know,' he said.

Indeed they were. A little crowd had fast become a rather large crowd as finally, *finally*, the ramp was lowered.

Only it wasn't a dark, sexy Russian that drove out, it was a very excited redhead who jerked the car out.

'The brakes…' she said.

The brakes were very highly strung and sensitive to pressure, but Nikolai didn't seem to care a bit as they bunny-hopped out.

'Where are we going?' she asked.

'Just follow the satnav.'

It was quite a drive through London. The car ran like silk and purred as it carried them through the night. They were on Northumberland Avenue and, at the roundabout, she followed instructions and turned onto The Mall.

'Are we going to Kensington Palace?' she asked when he refused to give her a clue.

'No.'

'Buckingham Palace, then,' she said. Oh, yes, she'd worked it out now. 'That's where Daniil and Sev met up. That's where—'

'We're not going to Buckingham Palace.'

Instead, they turned into Hans Place and it would seem that the destination was on her left and so Rachel parked, badly.

'Why are we here?'

There was a gentleman waiting to greet them and he wore a bright smile, despite the hour.

'Who is he?' Rachel asked, as he opened the door to a huge home.

'The real estate agent.'

'But they don't come out at one in the morning.' she said.

'They do for me.'

Of course they did, given the location!

There was no furniture and her heels clipped on the wooden floor. She looked up at the high ceilings and wrapped her arms around herself at the gorgeous feel to the house.

'This is the reception area...' the real estate agent said, and Rachel stepped into the vast room with luxurious drapes—there was a fireplace that she would just love to see with a lit fire in it. There was a huge chandelier that didn't look so huge in such a fine setting. It sparkled and cast such a lovely glow that she stared up at it.

'Does the house come with matching earrings?' she sighed.

'Excuse me?' the real estate agent checked, and Nikolai smiled as the man spoke on. 'You would have access to Hans Gardens and the tennis court...'

'Ha-ha,' Rachel said and peered out at the gardens through the lovely French windows. 'I can't imagine you playing tennis, Nikolai.'

They went through to the library and then the kitchen and down to the cool cellar.

Then they climbed a stunning staircase and there were just too many rooms and too much to see, but her heart was soaring. If he was thinking of buying this, then surely it meant that he'd be spending some time in London.

But she didn't want to get ahead of herself.

'Is this an investment property?' she, oh, so casually, asked him as she peered into the master bedroom.

'Could you wait outside?' Nikolai said to the real estate agent.

'I'll wait downstairs,' he said.

'No,' Nikolai corrected. 'You'll wait outside.'

Rachel stood at the window. The views were to die for, and she heard the front door close.

'You mustn't be so abrupt with people,' she admonished, looking at the poor real estate agent on his phone by the car. 'Couldn't he have waited in the kitchen or something?'

'Rachel,' Nikolai said, 'I don't want an audience for this.'

'For what?'

'I'm buying this house because I want to live here.'

'You're staying?' Hope soared, it really did. They didn't have to end just yet. 'But what about the yacht?'

'It will be nice for holidays but I don't think a yacht is a place to raise a baby.'

'Nikolai?' Rachel couldn't breathe, not big breaths anyway. She was trying to slow down her brain because it was leaping ahead and jumping to impossible conclusions. They were standing in a home that he wanted to buy and talking babies. Rachel was too scared to glimpse the dream. She was jerking the reins on her mind, trying to pull it back from a sudden gallop towards the future, sure that in a moment she'd tumble, that any second now he'd explain about some Russian supermodel he was dating on the side or some...

Her top teeth bit into her lip and he could see the confusion in her eyes.

'Look at the mantelpiece.'

Above the fire there was a small velvet box and Rachel frowned. 'What is it?'

'What do you think it is?'

'I don't know.' She did know. She thought it looked like an engagement ring, a massive emerald, high set and glinting in its box.

She didn't want to say anything, just in case she'd got it all wrong.

'Is it a ring for the supermodel?' she asked.

'What supermodel?'

'The one I just conjured up in my mind,' she admitted. 'The real love of your life.'

'You're the love of my life.'

'I don't believe you.' It was the most horrible tease, it had to be. Rachel pointed out the facts.

'We don't do relationships!'

'We're getting married,' Nikolai responded in his oh, so matter-of-fact way.

'Er...aren't you supposed to ask me?'

'I don't have to ask.'

He didn't.

'You're supposed to get down on bended knee,' she said.

'You can if you want.'

He came over and they were almost at eye level with each other, and she put her hands around his neck and smiled.

She was starting to believe it might be true.

'I thought you were leaving tomorrow.'

'No.'

'But you said that you were going to France.'

'*We're* going to France,' Nikolai said. 'For Anya's opening night in Paris. You can write your blog...'

'But when did you decide all this?' She was honestly bewildered, the news utterly unexpected. She had braced herself for his leaving and now he was saying they would be together for life. 'You told me on Saturday that you were leaving.'

'And even as I said it, I knew I was making a mistake. Rachel, I have never wanted one person or one place. The thought of waking up to the same view each day has never appealed and yet now...' He never showed weakness, it was how he had come to survive after all, but his one true weakness was Rachel and she was also his strength. She had revealed herself to him and he would open himself to her too. 'I want to wake up to you each morning, I want to see the seasons from one place. I want friends and I want family and I want a home, but only now do I believe that dream is possible, and it is only possible with you.'

He took the ring from the box and placed it on her finger.

'I love you,' he said. 'I think I did the day we met.'

'You left me in bed!' she pointed out.

'Because I didn't want the woman I was falling in love with to know about my past, yet it turns out that you knew already.'

'I was horrible when you told me.' Rachel thought back to the vodka bar and she still cringed at her handling of things that day.

'Because of what had happened to you,' Nikolai said.

'I never got my liquorice ice cream.' She pouted but he did not smile.

He was serious.

'Rachel, we're going to work on things but I promise you this—I don't care if you fall asleep with all the lights blazing just so long as you sleep by my side. And I will never wake you for sex or—'

Rachel interrupted him then. 'We can work on that one.'

'We shall.'

They could smile together about even the hardest things, and that was love, she knew.

'Can we elope?' she asked.

'We can.'

'Can we marry at sea?'

'I'd like that.'

It was better than either had dared dream.

EPILOGUE

'RACHEL, I JUST don't understand.'

Libby was perplexed!

Then again, her best friend had just told her she had run away to sea and was about to get married.

In ten minutes' time!

'You and Nikolai?'

'Yes. The celebrant has just been choppered in…'

'But where are you?'

'Just off the South of France,' Rachel said.

'I want to be there.'

'Yes, and my mother would get all offended and then if she came she'd insist on Aunty Mary and then Shona…'

'I get it.' Libby laughed.

'Nikolai would probably feed André to the sharks, so it's safer this way.'

'What are you wearing?'

'It's completely over the top, and I think you're going to tell me off. Remember my *Swan Lake* costume, the one I loved?'

'The one they lost.'

'They didn't lose it,' Rachel confessed. 'It fell into my bag!'

Yes, she could be bad, but she used it for good. She stood at the computer and when she came into view Libby gasped.

Rachel wore her very favourite costume, but with bare legs and her hair down and in ringlets. She had on loads of coral lipstick with lashings of mascara and no foundation, but it was her smile that made Libby gasp. She had never seen her friend truly happy or more re-laxed.

'Nikolai suits you.'

'Oh, he does.'

'I'm so happy for you.'

'I'm so happy for me.'

They said goodbye and then Rachel headed up from the master suite to the main deck.

Nikolai had had her tucked away all day and now she saw why.

No, she wasn't a flowers girl, so the deck was strewn with white feathers that blew and swirled in the breeze and she walked towards him to the sound of a harp, but played beautifully this time.

Theirs was a very deep and private love and they celebrated it quietly today.

'You look beautiful,' Nikolai said to his happy swan.

'So do you.'

He wore a dark suit, the off-the-peg suit that he had worn on the day they had met, and it was how she had first loved him.

Only today his eyes were not hidden behind dark glasses.

There was nothing to hide from now.

It was a short service but loaded with love.

'You are the best thing that ever happened in my life,' Nikolai said as he slipped a ring on her finger. 'I will love you for ever.'

And Yuri popped into her head then, a man who had been like a father to Nikolai and who had missed his wife so much after she had died. She thought how lovely it would be to spend every day, down to her last, with Nikolai.

To know him each day just a little more.

She felt like Odette for the first time.

And then it was her turn and she pushed her ring onto his finger and for ever it would remain there. And she didn't have to hold back from what she wanted to say, because there were three words this playboy now wanted to hear.

'I love you.'

That was it—they were husband and wife.

They were family.

She kissed the groom and he tasted divine.

And after.

They lay in the sky lounge and watched the montage and finally he saw her dance. They ate lobster Mornay with a huge side of caviar, and drank vodka infused with ginger.

And then his butler brought in cake.

They held the knife together and cut into the icing.

No marzipan.

Instead, shiny grey oozed out.

Liquorice ice cream!

Oh, it was worth waiting for and later they lay under the stars and kissed with black tongues and then she looked deeply into brown eyes that had melted the hard-est heart.

'My icebreaker,' Rachel said.

'Always.'

* * * * *

Don't miss the stunning conclusion to
IRRESISTIBLE RUSSIAN TYCOONS *in*
RETURN OF THE UNTAMED BILLIONAIRE
Available June 2016

And in case you missed it,
you can find out where it all started in
THE PRICE OF HIS REDEMPTION
THE COST OF THE FORBIDDEN
Available now!

MILLS & BOON®
Hardback – May 2016

ROMANCE

Morelli's Mistress	Anne Mather
A Tycoon to Be Reckoned With	Julia James
Billionaire Without a Past	Carol Marinelli
The Shock Cassano Baby	Andie Brock
The Most Scandalous Ravensdale	Melanie Milburne
The Sheikh's Last Mistress	Rachael Thomas
Claiming the Royal Innocent	Jennifer Hayward
Kept at the Argentine's Command	Lucy Ellis
The Billionaire Who Saw Her Beauty	Rebecca Winters
In the Boss's Castle	Jessica Gilmore
One Week with the French Tycoon	Christy McKellen
Rafael's Contract Bride	Nina Milne
Tempted by Hollywood's Top Doc	Louisa George
Perfect Rivals...	Amy Ruttan
English Rose in the Outback	Lucy Clark
A Family for Chloe	Lucy Clark
The Doctor's Baby Secret	Scarlet Wilson
Married for the Boss's Baby	Susan Carlisle
Twins for the Texan	Charlene Sands
Secret Baby Scandal	Joanne Rock

MILLS & BOON®
Large Print – May 2016

ROMANCE

The Queen's New Year Secret	Maisey Yates
Wearing the De Angelis Ring	Cathy Williams
The Cost of the Forbidden	Carol Marinelli
Mistress of His Revenge	Chantelle Shaw
Theseus Discovers His Heir	Michelle Smart
The Marriage He Must Keep	Dani Collins
Awakening the Ravensdale Heiress	Melanie Milburne
His Princess of Convenience	Rebecca Winters
Holiday with the Millionaire	Scarlet Wilson
The Husband She'd Never Met	Barbara Hannay
Unlocking Her Boss's Heart	Christy McKellen

HISTORICAL

In Debt to the Earl	Elizabeth Rolls
Rake Most Likely to Seduce	Bronwyn Scott
The Captain and His Innocent	Lucy Ashford
Scoundrel of Dunborough	Margaret Moore
One Night with the Viking	Harper St. George

MEDICAL

A Touch of Christmas Magic	Scarlet Wilson
Her Christmas Baby Bump	Robin Gianna
Winter Wedding in Vegas	Janice Lynn
One Night Before Christmas	Susan Carlisle
A December to Remember	Sue MacKay
A Father This Christmas?	Louisa Heaton

MILLS & BOON®
Hardback – June 2016

ROMANCE

Bought for the Greek's Revenge	Lynne Graham
An Heir to Make a Marriage	Abby Green
The Greek's Nine-Month Redemption	Maisey Yates
Expecting a Royal Scandal	Caitlin Crews
Return of the Untamed Billionaire	Carol Marinelli
Signed Over to Santino	Maya Blake
Wedded, Bedded, Betrayed	Michelle Smart
The Surprise Conti Child	Tara Pammi
The Greek's Nine-Month Surprise	Jennifer Faye
A Baby to Save Their Marriage	Scarlet Wilson
Stranded with Her Rescuer	Nikki Logan
Expecting the Fellani Heir	Lucy Gordon
The Prince and the Midwife	Robin Gianna
His Pregnant Sleeping Beauty	Lynne Marshall
One Night, Twin Consequences	Annie O'Neil
Twin Surprise for the Single Doc	Susanne Hampton
The Doctor's Forbidden Fling	Karin Baine
The Army Doc's Secret Wife	Charlotte Hawkes
A Pregnancy Scandal	Kat Cantrell
A Bride for the Boss	Maureen Child

MILLS & BOON®
Large Print – June 2016

ROMANCE

Leonetti's Housekeeper Bride	Lynne Graham
The Surprise De Angelis Baby	Cathy Williams
Castelli's Virgin Widow	Caitlin Crews
The Consequence He Must Claim	Dani Collins
Helios Crowns His Mistress	Michelle Smart
Illicit Night with the Greek	Susanna Carr
The Sheikh's Pregnant Prisoner	Tara Pammi
Saved by the CEO	Barbara Wallace
Pregnant with a Royal Baby!	Susan Meier
A Deal to Mend Their Marriage	Michelle Douglas
Swept into the Rich Man's World	Katrina Cudmore

HISTORICAL

Marriage Made in Rebellion	Sophia James
A Too Convenient Marriage	Georgie Lee
Redemption of the Rake	Elizabeth Beacon
Saving Marina	Lauri Robinson
The Notorious Countess	Liz Tyner

MEDICAL

Playboy Doc's Mistletoe Kiss	Tina Beckett
Her Doctor's Christmas Proposal	Louisa George
From Christmas to Forever?	Marion Lennox
A Mummy to Make Christmas	Susanne Hampton
Miracle Under the Mistletoe	Jennifer Taylor
His Christmas Bride-to-Be	Abigail Gordon

MILLS & BOON®

Why shop at millsandboon.co.uk?

Each year, thousands of romance readers find their perfect read at millsandboon.co.uk. That's because we're passionate about bringing you the very best romantic fiction. Here are some of the advantages of shopping at www.millsandboon.co.uk:

* **Get new books first**—you'll be able to buy your favourite books one month before they hit the shops

* **Get exclusive discounts**—you'll also be able to buy our specially created monthly collections, with up to 50% off the RRP

* **Find your favourite authors**—latest news, interviews and new releases for all your favourite authors and series on our website, plus ideas for what to try next

* **Join in**—once you've bought your favourite books, don't forget to register with us to rate, review and join in the discussions

Visit **www.millsandboon.co.uk** for all this and more today!